McLEAN KNOWS
THE ANSWERS

The famous Inspector McLean of Scotland
Yard is in action again, solving sixteen cases
including murder, kidnapping and fraud.
They have all the quick and vivid action
associated with the detective's exploits and
will not disappoint McLean's many fans.

D1114082

McLEAN KNOWS
THE ANSWERS

McLEAN KNOWS THE ANSWERS

by

George Goodchild

DOURO - DUMMER PUBLIC LIBRARY
DISCARDED

Dales Large Print Books
Long Preston, North Yorkshire,
BD23 4ND, England.

British Library Cataloguing in Publication Data.

Goodchild, George
    McLean knows the answers.

    A catalogue record of this book is
    available from the British Library

    ISBN   1-84262-214-5 pbk

First published in Great Britain in 1967
by John Long Limited

Copyright © George Goodchild 1967

The moral right of the author has been asserted

Published in Large Print 2003 by arrangement with
Mrs S Roberts

All Rights reserved. No part of this publication may be
reproduced, stored in a retrieval system, or transmitted in any
form or by any means, electronic, mechanical, photocopying,
recording or otherwise without the prior permission of the
Copyright owner.

Dales Large Print is an imprint of Library Magna Books Ltd.

Printed and bound in Great Britain by
T.J. (International) Ltd., Cornwall, PL28 8RW

Contents

Contents

1

Mrs Willington's Secret

I

On his occasional trips to the coast from London, Inspector McLean had often admired the big house high up in the woods above the main road between Esher and Guildford. He had no idea what it was called or who lived there for its approach was on a side road.

But on a sunny morning in June he was destined to know more about it for he was called into the office of his Chief and informed that a woman named Mrs Willington who lived near Guildford had been found dead in her bed the previous morning, and the county police were asking for help in the investigation. It was assumed that she had died from an overdose of sleeping tablets, but the post-mortem which had taken place the previous night did not support that probability.

Half an hour later Inspector McLean, accompanied by his assistant, Sergeant Brook were on the road, bound for county police headquarters. Arriving there McLean saw an Inspector Simpson whom he knew well.

'A top-grade affair,' Simpson said. 'Her husband John Willington is a big shot in the property market. She's his second wife, and about twenty years younger. They have a flat in town and another place in Paris. She was found at eight o'clock yesterday morning in bed – dead.'

'Who found her?' McLean asked.

'Her personal maid, a French girl named Yvonne. She took her a cup of tea. On the bedside table she found an empty bottle which had contained sleeping pills. It was at first presumed that she had taken an overdose, but the post-mortem found that although she had certainly taken some pills, the amount traced was not enough to cause death. The doctor who had prescribed them said he had last given her a prescription for twenty of the tablets only four days previously, and had she taken the whole lot in one dose they could not have harmed her. Otherwise her health was quite good. All that was wrong with her was that she worried too much.'

'About what?'

'Nothing which could be discovered. She was apparently happily married to a rich man, and lived in a gorgeous house when she was not at the expensive London flat.'

'Was her husband at the house when this happened?'

'No. He spent the night in Liverpool where he has some business connections. We telephoned him at once and he arrived yesterday afternoon. But he's there now – a very worried man.'

McLean was taken to see the body shortly afterwards. It was that of a woman about forty years of age. Her face looked as if it was moulded in wax, and there was no doubt that in her youth she had been very beautiful.

'Can you say approximately at what time she died?' McLean asked the pathologist who was present.

'Somewhere between ten and eleven o'clock on Thursday night.'

Later McLean and Brook were piloted to the house where the tragedy had taken place. Inspector Simpson drove his own car and some miles down the main road his winking traffic signal indicted that he was turning into a narrow lane on his left.

11

'That's curious,' McLean said. 'I believe he is going to that big house on the hill. I've often wondered who had the good fortune to own it.'

It was soon clear that McLean was right, for at the end of the lane there was a pair of wrought-iron gates, and a signboard marked Harpford House. Simpson turned through the open gates, and Brook followed. A twisting drive through resplendent gardens brought them to a wide terrace in front of the handsome edifice where the two cars pulled up, and the occupants got out.

'I'll introduce you to Willington,' Simpson said. 'And then I'll have to leave you as I have an appointment with the Coroner.'

A ring at the bell brought a young and well-dressed woman to the door. Simpson gave her a smile of recognition and said he wished to see Mr Willington. They sat in the wide and splendidly furnished hall while she went to deliver the message. A few moments later she came back and took them to a room overlooking the rear part of the beautiful garden, where a bearded man of about sixty years of age was sitting at a table. He rose and nodded to Simpson.

'You wished to see me, Inspector?' he asked.

'Yes, sir. I have to inform you that the case has gone to London, and these two officers are taking over. This is Inspector McLean – and Sergeant Brook from Scotland Yard.'

Willington nodded and shook their hands. Simpson then apologised for having to leave at once, and when the door was closed behind him Willington begged them to be seated.

'I'm glad you have taken over, Inspector,' he said. 'This is a complete mystery to me. It doesn't make any kind of sense at all.'

'Did you know that your wife was taking sleeping pills?' McLean asked.

'Yes. She suffered a great deal from insomnia. Her doctor prescribed them, and she benefited from them. She took one usually, but two occasionally, in a glass of milk before retiring for the night.'

'Was this insomnia due to any particular cause?'

'None that I could discover. She used to complain about being lonely, and I must confess that I am away from home a great deal, but never for long periods.'

'Were you away on the night when she died?'

'Yes. I went up to Liverpool the previous day to look at some property in which I was interested. Actually I telephoned her that evening to tell her that it was necessary for me to spend another night up there. She seemed to be quite happy then, and even cracked a joke with me.'

'Where did you stay in Liverpool?'

'At the Majestic. It's one of my properties.'

'Did you have anyone with you – your secretary or chauffeur?'

'No. I left the chauffeur here for my wife's convenience. He has a flat over the garage. There was no need for my secretary.'

'Who was the young lady who showed me in?'

'My wife's personal maid. Her name is Yvonne Deschamps. We brought her from Paris five years ago after my marriage. I should tell you that my first wife died eight years ago.'

'I should like to ask the young woman some questions,' McLean said.

'Certainly. I'll go and find her and will send her here.'

II

A few moments later there was a rap on the door and Yvonne entered. She spoke very good English but with a strong French accent. In reply to McLean's questions she said that she had taken a glass of milk to Mrs Willington's bedroom on the night in question, and that Mrs Willington had sat up with her watching television until shortly before ten o'clock, when she said 'good night' and retired.

'When you were in her room did you see the bottle containing the sleeping pills?' McLean asked.

'No. She always got them herself from the top drawer of the dressing table. I usually found the bottle in the morning on the bedside table.'

'Did you see that bottle on the previous morning?'

'Yes.'

'Can you say how many tablets there were in it then?'

'No. It was a blue bottle and the glass was very thick, but I took the prescription to the chemist two days previously and I know it was marked "20 tablets, one to be taken when needed".'

'For how long had she been taking these tablets?' McLean asked.

'For the past two or three months.'

'Not previous to that?'

'No.'

'On the night in question did she appear to be quite normal?'

'She was rather quieter – quieter than usual.'

'Do you sleep close to her room?'

'Only two doors away. If she needed me she had only to push a bell beside her bed. She never locked her door.'

'Did her husband treat her well?'

'Oh yes. He always telephoned her when he was away from home – even one night.'

Willington returned soon after McLean had dismissed her, and McLean then said he would like to see the dead woman's room.

'I know it was sealed by the county police,' McLean said. 'But I have the key.'

'Then please go up,' Willington said. 'It is the third door on the right at the top of the staircase.'

McLean and Brook mounted the wide staircase, on the walls of which were some large and valuable paintings by old masters. The room itself was rather ostentatious, with casement windows leading to a covered balcony. A vast wardrobe was full of feminine clothing, all comparatively new. One of the oil paintings was of Mrs

16

Willington herself, some years younger, done by a famous portrait painter. There was a communicating door to the next bedroom. It had been bolted on McLean's side. McLean drew the bolt aside and saw a dressing gown hanging on the door and a pair of large slippers under the bedside table.

'Willington's room presumably,' he said. 'Not quite so exotic as his wife's.'

From the balcony there was a splendid view of the upper gardens in which was a wide circular pool with a central fountain, but the fountain was not now in action, and the crystal clear water was like a mirror. From the water came a ray of reflected light. It was a combination of silver and gold, and it never moved.

'Looks like a dead goldfish,' he said to Brook. 'We'll have a look at it later. Let's get back into the bedroom. I want to have a look in those numerous drawers.'

The ensuing search produced a lot of odd but inexpensive jewellery, and some letters from various friends, but nothing of real interest was found, and when finally they left the room McLean locked it up and they went downstairs and into the garden towards the pool. Here McLean made an

17

interesting discovery. The pool contained not only one dead goldfish, but three in different places, and all the others looked unusually sluggish.

'They're sick to death, literally,' he mused. 'Get one of the dead ones out, Brook.'

Brook quickly retrieved one of the fishes. It bore no injury of any kind and appeared to be quite young and healthy.

'Curious,' McLean said. 'I believe they have been poisoned. See if you can find a drain tap anywhere. There is only about two feet of water, and there must be a sump to hold the fish when the water is drained off.'

The drain tap was soon found, and McLean turned it to its full extent, and very soon watched the water level getting lower and lower.

'I can now see the sump,' he said. 'It should not take very long to empty.'

They sat on a nearby seat and had a smoke until the water had drained off, leaving only the sump for the fishes to flounder in. McLean then stepped down on to the wet concrete, peering at its surface as he walked around.

'What are we looking for?' Brook asked.

'Pills or tablets. I don't think they would completely dissolve in this cold water. Ah, here are two!'

He stooped and picked up two partially dissolved white tablets. Then Brook found another, and finally they had fourteen between them.

'Get the water turned on, Brook,' McLean said, 'or we shall have some more casualties.'

Brook turned on the tap and then rejoined McLean who was placing the sodden tablets into an empty matchbox.

'What do you make of it?' Brook asked.

'Murder,' McLean said. 'It was made to look as if Mrs Willington had taken all the tablets in that bottle. We know that she took one or perhaps two, but it was the murderer who took the rest away with him, and threw them into the fish pool on his way from the house.'

'In that case how did she die?' Brook asked.

'That's a difficult question. Had she been strangled it would have shown up. My own feeling is that she was suffocated – not difficult to do with a pillow pressed hard down on her nose and mouth. But theorising won't help us much. We'll get these tablets and that dead fish along to the forensic department, and then I'll check up

19

Willington's statement.'

From county police headquarters McLean telephoned the hotel in Liverpool where Willington said he had stayed. He was informed that there was no doubt about this, for on the night in question he was seen by several members of the staff up to nearly midnight.

'That puts him in the clear,' McLean said. 'We have to look nearer home.'

III

McLean and Brook were at the big house early the next morning where in the first place they saw Willington again. When he was told that murder was strongly suspected he gazed at McClean incredulously.

'But nobody had cause to harm her,' he said.

'Had she any money in her own right?' McLean asked.

'Yes. On our marriage I made over to her some shares in my various companies worth today about £50,000.'

'Did she ever make a will?'

'I think she did some months ago. It may be at her bank or with her solicitor.'

McLean saw the will later at a local bank. It was in a sealed envelope which was opened when McLean produced his warrant. It was dated only a few months earlier, and one of the witnesses was Yvonne Deschamps. Mrs Willington left all her estate to Edward Arthur Molyneux of an address in Paris.

'Now we are really on to something,' he told Brook. 'Mademoiselle Deschamps has a lot of questions to answer.'

He saw Yvonne later in her own sitting-room. She did not look very happy which was natural in the circumstances, but McLean swiftly caused her to look even less happy.

'Did you know Mrs Willington before she engaged you as her personal maid?' he asked.

'Yes. I used to look after her flat in Paris.'

'Did you know a man named Molyneux?'

'Yes,' she said. 'He used to call at the flat.'

'Has he ever been here?'

She seemed to hesitate, and McLean was quick to take her up.

'You must answer that question,' he said. 'For it is very important.'

'Yes,' she said. 'He has called here several times recently.'

'When was he last here?'

'It – it was on Tuesday morning.'

'After Mr Willington went to Liverpool?'

'Yes.'

'And on the previous occasions did he ever meet Mr Willington?'

'No.'

From her increasing nervousness McLean knew she was keeping something back.

'When you witnessed the will made by Mrs Willington did you notice any of the details?'

'No. I just signed my name below another person's.'

'You did not know that Mrs Willington left her entire estate to this Mr Molyneux?' McLean asked.

She stared speechlessly at McLean, and then shook her head. On the verge of tears she began to say something and then stopped.

'Tell me what you were about to say,' McLean said. 'I must warn you this is a case of murder.'

'Oh no,' she cried hysterically. 'There must be a mistake. I'll tell you all I know. Mr Molyneux is Madam's illegitimate son. She never married because the boy's father was killed in the war. When she met Mr

Willington the boy was away at school and she feared that if she told him the truth about the boy it might ruin her chance of making a fortunate marriage. She had been sending him money for a long time, but a few months ago she learned that he was in England, and from that time she has been very worried. She knew that her secret was safe with me, but I told her that it would be better if she confessed to her husband. She could never bring herself to do that.'

'How old is the son now?'

'Twenty-two.'

'Do you know where he can be found?'

'Not the address, but Madam used to telephone him at Temple Bar 27642.'

'Did he know that he was named as the sole beneficiary in her will.'

'I don't know. She may have told him when they were together, as there were many times when Mr Willington was away on business.'

McLean finally thanked her and then hurried back to London where he got in touch with the appropriate telephone exchange. He was told that the owner of the telephone number was Mrs Young. The address was a flat in the Covent Garden area.

'Let's go, Brook,' he said.

A few minutes later they were ringing the bell of the flat on the first floor. A young and rather swarthy man came to the door. He bore a striking resemblance to the dead woman, and McLean had no doubt about his identity.

'Mr Molyneux?' McLean asked.

'Yes. What is your business?'

'I am a police officer, and think you may be able to help me. May we come in?'

'Yes, but I am only a visitor here. The flat was sublet to me by the owner – Mrs Young – who has gone abroad.'

'When did you last see your mother?' McLean asked.

'My mother?'

'Yes, Mrs Willington.'

'It was on Tuesday last. She telephoned me and invited me to call on her.'

'For any particular reason?'

'No. Just for a chat. I presume you know that I am her natural son?'

'I do. Did you help her to keep that fact from Mr Willington?'

'Naturally. She has supported me all these years, and I didn't want to spoil things for her.'

'Do you know that she was found dead in

her bed two days ago?'

'No,' he gasped. 'When I saw her on Tuesday she looked well enough, although she told me she had been sleeping badly.'

McLean, whose eagle gaze never missed anything, reached out for a newspaper which was lying in a chair. Uppermost was the heading in heavy type, RICH WOMAN'S DEATH MYSTERY. Three inches of letterpress followed.

'It's curious that you should have missed this,' McLean said and held the news item under Molyneux's nose.

'I saw the headline, but didn't know it referred to my mother,' he said. 'Had I read further I should have got in touch with the police.'

'I find it a little difficult to believe that,' McLean said. 'Now I must ask you to come with us to police headquarters for further questioning.'

At headquarters McLean lost no time in getting a search warrant on the flat. There he and Brook went through Molyneux's rather scant luggage. The two suitcases contained nothing of interest, but in the pocket of a jacket was a hundred pounds in five-pound notes.

'Got from his mother on Tuesday, I

imagine,' McLean said. 'They don't help much. Try that lounge suit while I go through the bureau.'

While McLean was looking at a passport which he had found in the bureau Brook made an ejaculation which brought McLean's head round.

'Have you found something?' McLean asked.

'Only a bus ticket in a side pocket which has a hole in it. Something seems to have gone through the hole into the lining. Feels like a sixpence.'

McLean took the coat and turned the pocket inside out. He saw the hole and then felt the small object between the lining and the cloth proper. With a penknife he opened the hole sufficiently to get his fingers through, and ultimately retrieved the article. It was a hard white round tablet exactly like those taken from the fishpond.

'I think we've got him, Brook,' he said. 'Keep that bus ticket. It may help to sew up this case. Now drive back to headquarters.'

Later it was established that the tablet was identical with those found by McLean in the fishpond, and that the bus ticket was issued late on the night when Mrs Willington died. The owner had travelled from the railway station some two miles away to a bus stop quite close to Willington's house. The conductor on the bus described Molyneux very accurately, and said he would be able to recognise him again. This he did subsequently, to Molyneux's obvious discomfiture.

It was when Molyneux was personally searched that McLean found in one of his pockets a brand-new key which was found to fit one of the doors of the big house.

'I think that's why he called on the Tuesday,' McLean said. 'To make an impression of the key, and get one cut. Well, he played for big stakes without regard for the fact that his victim was to be his own mother. Weep no tears for him, Brook.'

'Not me,' Brook said. 'I'm going to buy myself a nice long drink.'

'I'll think I'll join you,' McLean said.

2

The Kidnappers

I

At shortly after midnight on a chill November evening Inspector McLean and Sergeant Brook left Scotland Yard in a fast car to go to a house in Highgate in response to an urgent call from a Dr Howlett who reported that he had been called to the house in question by the tenant – a Mrs Rothman – who had returned from a party to find her two-year-old baby gone, and its nurse so badly drugged that at the moment she was unable to make a statement.

When they reached the house and McLean pushed the bell button the door was opened by a tall sombre man, who peered at the callers.

'I'm Dr Howlett,' he said. 'I presume you are from the police. Please come in. The lady of the house – Mrs Rothman – is too upset at the moment to be seen. I have given her a sedative to quieten her in the meantime. I have managed to bring the nurse to her senses. This way.'

He led them through the hall and up the broad staircase to a room on the first floor. Here McLean found a young woman, lying on a bed, and clad in a dressing-gown over a sleeping suit. Away in the corner was a child's cot, with the bedclothes awry, and two cuddly dolls lying close to the silk pillow. Over all was a pungent smell of chloroform.

'She was badly doped,' the doctor said. 'I'm not sure whether she should go to hospital, but I should know shortly.'

'Has she explained what happened?' McLean asked.

'Not yet. Mrs Rothman says her name is Millicent Walters, and that she has been in her employ ever since the little girl was born – two years ago. She had excellent references and was very devoted to the child. I can well believe that for there is evidence that she put up considerable resistance. I think she may be in a state now to explain matters.'

McLean went closer to the bed. The girl's eyes were open, and the pupils greatly enlarged, her breathing was heavy, but not so heavy as to impede her speech. McLean noticed that there was a graze on her bottom jaw, and that one of the sleeves of her dressing-gown was almost torn off.

'I am a police officer,' he said quietly. 'Do you feel well enough to answer some questions?'

'Yes,' she replied in a weak voice. 'Is – is baby all right?'

'I'm afraid not. She was taken away.'

'Oh,' she moaned. 'I did my best, but it was useless.'

'You mustn't worry,' McLean said. 'You were not to blame in the least. Tell me what happened.'

'Madam told me she would be late home, and I went to bed about ten o'clock. It was at half past eleven when I was awakened by a gentle knocking on the door. I thought it was Madam, and got up and unlatched the door. There were two men outside, wearing dark overcoats, and nylon stockings stretched over their heads. One was very tall but the other was much smaller. The taller man told me that if I got back into bed and behaved myself nothing would happen to me. I thought they were just burglars, but as I backed towards the bed the other man went towards the cot and then I realised it was the baby they wanted. I dodged past the tall man and reached the dressing-table where I had left a pair of large cutting-out scissors. The shorter man was just taking baby into his arms when I struck him in the shoulder with the point of the scissors. He dropped the baby and gave a howl of pain, but the next moment the tall man caught me by the throat and what happened is all very hazy. I think I was hit on the jaw, and then carried to the bed. My – my head aches rather badly.'

'I won't worry you any more at the moment,' McLean said. 'I'm sure you'll soon feel much better. Just rest quietly.'

Outside the bedroom door the doctor explained that he had only been to the house once previously to attend a daily maid who had cut her hand badly. He believed that Mrs Rothman was a widow and that she had rented the house about a year previously. He himself lived only a hundred yards away.

'At what time did Mrs Rothman ring you?' McLean asked.

'Just before midnight. I hadn't gone to bed, and left instantly. She was in a terrible state – almost hysterical. I gave her a mild sedative and told her I would telephone the

31

police and let her know when you arrived. I think by now she may be slightly more composed. If you will wait downstairs I'll bring her down.'

A few minutes later the doctor brought Mrs Rothman into the reception room where McLean and Brook were waiting. She was a strikingly good-looking woman of about thirty years of age, but her eyes were red and swollen from weeping and she wore a short mink coat over her evening gown. The doctor helped her into an easy chair, and then introduced McLean and Brook.

'I must get back to my patient,' he said. 'I think there is no need to take her to the hospital. All she needs is rest.'

'I'm sorry to have to disturb you, madam,' McLean said when the door closed on the doctor. 'The nurse has been revived and has made a statement. Two men were involved in this business, and the girl put up a strong resistance until she was overcome and doped. Can you help us at all in this matter?'

'I wish I could, but I am completely in the dark. It would make sense if I were a rich woman, but my husband died just over a year ago, and left me very, very little. I had to sell our old house to pay off the mortgage, and then get myself a job.'

'What kind of job?' McLean asked.

'Receptionist to a dental surgeon in Wimpole Street.'

'At what time did you leave here this evening?'

'Seven o'clock. I went to a party given by an old friend of mine – Mrs Burnside of 7 Cross Lanes, Hampstead. I told Millicent the nurse where I was going.'

'Are there any other servants in the house?'

'No. There's a woman who comes in daily to do the chores. I can't afford any other help.'

'Did she know that you were going to the party?'

'No, not unless Millicent told her.'

'I won't detain you any longer now,' McLean said. 'But I shall have to stay here a little longer to find out how the kidnappers got into the house. Can I help you to your room?'

'Thank you, but I can manage.'

When she had left McLean and Brook went upstairs again to find the doctor about to leave. He said the patient was much improved, and had no doubt she would sleep until the morning when he would call again.

'There's just one thing,' McLean said. 'I want to do some investigation here. Can we help you take the patient to another room?'

The doctor was agreeable, and the girl was transferred to the room next door.

II

'Now,' McLean said. 'Let's see how those two fellows managed to get into the house. They must have found the front door latched against them.'

The back door was found latched and bolted on the inside, but in the dining-room which had a french window looking out on to the garden there were signs that a jemmy or similar tool had been used to prise the windows apart.

'As easy as falling off a log,' Brook commented. 'The housebreaker's gift from heaven.'

They climbed the stairs again and entered the night nursery. The doctor had been careful not to alter the position of anything and on the floor near the cot McLean found the pair of long scissors which the doped girl had mentioned. They were bloodstained on the points. A fragile vase containing a sprig of mimosa had been knocked from a side table, and lay in pieces on the floor. Brook gathered them up.

'Quite a dog fight!' he commented.

It was in the communicating bathroom that McLean found something of interest. It was a cigarette-end, lying on the tiled window ledge. On the corked tip of it was the merest trace of lipstick.

'That's curious,' he said. 'We'll have to question the nurse about that in the morning. Well, there's nothing else we can do tonight. We'll resume our search outside that casement window in the light of day.'

When McLean and Brook reached the house on the following morning they found Mrs Rothman up and about, but looking as worried as any woman would be in the circumstances.

'I've heard nothing over the telephone,' she said. 'Not a word to explain this strange affair. Millicent is much better and wants to get up but I've told her she must wait and hear what the doctor says.'

'That was wise,' McLean said. 'Tell me – does Millicent smoke?'

'I don't think so. Certainly not in the house.'

'Does anyone else use the bathroom next

to the night nursery?'

'No, there is a second bathroom next to my bedroom.'

When, a little later, the daily help arrived McLean took up the cigarette matter with her.

'Yes. I do have a fag now and again,' she admitted, 'but never when I'm working.'

'I found this cigarette-end last night,' McLean said. 'It was on the window ledge of the nursery bathroom. Can you account for that?'

'No, I can't. I tidied up the bathrooms before I left yesterday morning,' she said. 'It wasn't there then.'

When the doctor arrived he pronounced that Millicent had completely recovered and that there was no need for him to call again. It was while McLean and Brook were examining the garden outside the casement window that she appeared on the terrace.

'Good morning,' McLean said. 'I'm glad to hear you are better. That was a nasty experience you had. Tell me a little more about the two men. Was there anything special about their voices? I mean any accent or dialect?'

'It was only the taller man who spoke. He had a cultured tone of voice, but with a trace of northern accent – Yorkshire or Lancashire. His companion never uttered a word.'

'But he cried out when you struck him with the scissors?'

'Yes, quite loudly.'

'Was it a shrill cry?'

'Yes – it was rather.'

'Do you think it might have been a woman dressed as a man?'

'I never thought of that,' she said. 'Yes, it might have been a woman. I noticed that his feet were very small, and he handled the baby in quite a feminine way.'

'Thank you,' McLean said. 'I presume you don't smoke?'

'No. I hate smoking.'

'That was smart of you, Inspector,' Brook said when she had entered the house.

'Not in the circumstances. It looks as if the woman went into the bathroom to attend to her injury, before the baby was removed. But let's get on with our work.'

The paving outside the window yielded no clue of any kind. McLean moved round the terrace to a place close to the main door, where a waiting car would naturally be parked. Here the short drive was hard and clean all the way to the entrance gate. On coming back to the front door McLean noticed a crumpled piece of buff-coloured paper lying in the boundary hedge. He retrieved it and straightened it out. It was an unused Pools envelope, and on the back of it was a short shopping list of domestic items. But on the front of it was something which caused McLean to catch his breath. It was the rubber-stamped number of the investor.

'Look at that, Brook,' he said. 'But don't shout yet. It may have been discarded by Mrs Rothman or someone else in the house. Let's go and find out.'

None of the three women in the house could explain how the envelope got there, and McLean's hopes were raised accordingly.

'It will be interesting to find out who owns that number,' he said to Brook. 'Let's get back to the office and get in touch with the Pools firm.'

The subsequent enquiry was made through the Liverpool police force, who promised an early reply.

'It's bound to take a little time,' McLean said. 'I propose to use that up by seeing the woman who invited Mrs Rothman to her party. Someone wanted that child badly, and not for ransom I think, or Mrs

Rothman would have heard from them before now.'

At the Hampstead house McLean asked to see Mrs Burnside, and was shown into a room where a pretty middle-aged woman was seated before a blazing log fire. She rose as they entered.

'I'm sorry to trouble you, madam,' McLean said. 'I have just come from the house of your friend, Mrs Rothman. Perhaps you may have heard from her?'

'Yes, indeed. I was shocked and astonished to hear what had happened there.'

'I believe you have known her for a long time?'

'Yes. We were at school together many years ago. She lost her husband soon after her baby was born.'

'Was it a happy marriage?'

'I thought so at first. They lived in good style – nothing but the best was good enough. Rothman had inherited a lot of money from his father who was a stockbroker, and was always buying new cars – even a small two-seater aeroplane, but after his death poor Phillipa discovered that he was hopelessly in debt. Fortunately the house was in her name, but that too was mortgaged. When she paid that off there

39

was precious little left, and she had to find a job and take a rented house.'

'What happened to her husband that he should die so young?'

'He had gone to Spain on some business matter, flying his own 'plane. He was a good pilot – ex-R.A.F. On the way home he ran into some sort of trouble, and later some bits of his 'plane were found in the sea. His body was never recovered.'

'That was over a year ago?'

'About eighteen months.'

'What sort of a man was he, physically?'

'Rather tall – over six feet. I wasn't able to go to their wedding which took place three years previously, but Phillipa sent me a photograph, if you'd care to see it.'

McLean said he would, and she produced a large album, and finally pointed to a photograph of the married couple, standing outside a country church.

McLean finally thanked her and then drove back to Scotland Yard. There they found a telephone message from the Liverpool police to the effect that the owner of the crumpled envelope was a Mr John Bayne of an address near Romsey in the New Forest.

'Now for Mr Bayne,' McLean said. 'He should prove interesting.'

III

There was some difficulty in finding Mr Bayne's house, for it lay in a clearing, in one of the most dense parts of the forest, half a mile off the main road, and the signpost which must have borne the name of the house had been broken off, leaving only a bare stump. They were finally directed to it by a local man.

When McLean rang the door-bell a beautiful dark-complexioned woman of about thirty years of age came to the door and stared rather hard at the visitors.

'Is Mr Bayne at home?' McLean asked.

'I am sor-ree,' she said, with a strong latin accent. 'He have gone into zee village to shop for me. I expect heem back soon. I am Mrs Bayne. Can I help?'

'I don't think so,' McLean said. 'I am a police officer and think he may be of assistance in a certain matter. I'll wait in the car for his return.'

'So,' she said. 'Excuse me if I close zee door. There is very cold wind.'

'There is indeed,' McLean said.

It was about ten minutes later when a big

saloon car appeared in the drive. The man who drove it stopped close to the police car, and then emerged, He was big and corpulent, and wore heavy horn-rimmed spectacles. McLean walked across to him.

'Mr Bayne?' he asked.

'Yes.'

'I am a police officer and think you may be able to help me in a certain investigation.'

'Most certainly, if I can.'

'Were you recently at Highgate, near Hampstead?'

'No, I have only been there once in my life, and that was years ago.'

McLean then produced the crumpled Pools envelope and showed it to him.

'Is that registration number yours?' he asked.

'I think it is, but I can't remember, as I haven't betted on the Pools for several months.'

'It was found in the drive of a house in Highgate. Can you suggest how it might have got there?'

'No, I can't. But I remember throwing some old Pools coupons into the dustbin recently. It might have blown away when the dustbin was emptied.'

'I don't think so,' McLean said. 'Can we

go inside the house. It's very cold out here.'

'Of course.'

McLean and Brook followed him to the door, and from there into a sitting-room. Here he removed his hat and flung it on to a couch. McLean, who was very close to him stared hard at his jet-black hair, and came to the quick conclusion that it was cunningly dyed.

'Is your wife Italian?' McLean asked.

'No, Spanish.'

'How long have you been married?'

'Five years.'

'Any children?'

'Only one – a girl of two years. But why all these strange questions?'

'Because I have reason to believe that your name is not John Bayne, but John Rothman, who was presumed to have died in an aeroplane accident eighteen months ago. Do you deny that?'

'Of course I deny it.'

'In that case I must ask you to come with me to be confronted by a person who will put that question beyond all doubt.'

'What person?'

'The woman whom I believe to be your wife, and who–'

He was interrupted by the Spanish

43

woman's sudden entrance into the room. She mumbled an apology, and turned to leave.

'Please stay, madam,' McLean said.

She came back, staggering a little. Brook pulled up a chair and she sank back in it, her face became contorted with obvious pain.

'That injury to your back must be still worrying you,' McLean said.

She sat upright now, staring at her alleged husband. He was silent for a few moments.

'Tell him, John,' she begged. 'It is no use – he knows.'

'All right,' he said. 'I lied, Inspector. I am John Rothman. Anita here is not my wife. My real wife and I never hit it off. I played ducks and drakes with the money my father left me. I got hopelessly into debt, and my firm was to be hammered on the Stock Exchange. But I had some money parked away secretly. I planned it all well in advance – crashed the 'plane into the sea a mile or two from land and swam ashore. I believed I could start a new life with Anita, but as time went on I missed that child badly. It became an obsession with me, and finally I discovered where my wife was living. Once or twice I saw the nursemaid out with the baby, but she gave me no opportunity to

44

take the child. I then decided to do what I did, but I needed Anita's help. She refused at first, but finally she consented, and you know the rest.'

'You realise you are open to several serious charges?'

'Yes. What do you want now?'

'I want you to promise you will stay here until I see you again.'

'Yes, but what about Anita?'

'Is the baby here?'

'Yes – asleep,' Anita said.

'I need your help to restore her to her mother immediately. Is that convenient?'

Anita said it was, and a few minutes later she came down the stairs, fully dressed, with the child still asleep. Again McLean warned Rothman, and then the car started off on the road to London. Anita wept a little on the journey but the baby slept like a log. To McLean the journey was most pleasant, for he had visions of Mrs Rothman's joy and delight when she discovered what they were bringing to her.

3

Death of a Water-skier

I

Major Munroe was entranced at the sight which met his gaze from the window of his bedroom at Radcliffe Hotel along the Helford River in South Cornwall. In the bright morning sunlight a young girl, as bronzed as a new penny, and wearing nothing but a bikini and swim-cap, was engaged in water-ski-ing. The speedboat to which she was attached was making terrific speed, and as it drew nearer the sound of the powerful engine almost deafened him.

The girl, beautifully poised, looked like a goddess, and it was clear to him that she was absolutely expert and complete master of the situation. He seized his binoculars to get a closer view of the spectacle, and now he could see that there were two men in the speedboat, one at the tiller and the other manipulating a cine-camera. The boat made three different runs, during which the skier executed every trick imaginable, with never a fault. Finally the boat and the skier disappeared from his view, and the Major resumed his shaving, and then went down to breakfast.

It was his first morning at the hotel, and it was natural that he should mention the skiing to the man at the opposite table during breakfast.

'Oh, her,' his fellow guest said. 'She's been doing that for the past week. She and her friends have rented a big house up the estuary. I think it's some film unit.'

On the following morning at about the same hour as previously the speedboat and the skier appeared again, and the Major was thrilled by his free entertainment. The sea was a shade rougher than on the previous day, but it seemed to make no difference to the skier. Through his binoculars the Major could see her gleaming white teeth and the smile of absolute composure on her face. But then the unexpected happened. She suddenly leaned sideways, let go of the tow-rope and fell into the sea. The skis fell off her feet, and the Major expected to see her swimming freely, but instead he only saw the floating skis and a bare arm above the water. The speedboat went round in a wide circle and then came back at great speed to the place where she had disappeared. They were still looking for her when the Major went downstairs to his breakfast. A little later his fellow guest at the neighbouring table joined him.

'Morning!' he said. 'There seems to have been an accident with that ski-ing crowd. I've just seen that girl fished out of the ocean.'

'I saw it happen,' the Major said. 'She lost her balance, and must have hit her head on a ski or something. They were a long time looking for her. Is she all right?'

'She looked far from all right. Anyway, when they got her aboard they went streaking up the estuary towards the house where they live.'

They were finishing their breakfast when a party of men who had gone out very early on a fishing trip entered the breakfast room. The Major pricked up his ears at the conversation which he could not fail to overhear.

'She looked dead to me,' one of them said. 'They had to carry her into the house.'

'But she was a splendid swimmer,' another said. 'I've seen her in the water several times.'

'Excuse me,' the Major interjected. 'But

are you talking about the water-ski-ing girl?'

'That's right. We were fishing about half a mile from the house when they brought her ashore. Do you know her?'

'No, but I saw her go into the sea. She didn't appear to make any attempt at swimming.'

'Then you'd better get in touch with the police. If she's dead your evidence may be useful.'

'I'll do that,' the Major said.

It was on the following morning that Inspector McLean at Scotland Yard was called into the office of his Chief and instructed to leave at once for Falmouth to investigate the strange death of the water-skier.

'Her name is Laura Banting,' his Chief said. 'She and a party of friends rented a house up the Helford River. It is called Tideways. At first it looked like an accident, but when they got her body into the boat which was towing her they found a bullet wound in her breast. You had better go by air, and I'll arrange to have a car meet you at the nearest airport.'

An hour later McLean, accompanied by his assistant, Sergeant Brook, was a mile up in the air making for the west country. To

Brook, who was born in that part of the country, this was more in the nature of a holiday than grim business.

'May be a long investigation – I hope,' he said.

'Have a heart,' McLean remonstrated. 'This is murder.'

On reaching Falmouth McLean found a very luxurious police car waiting to take them to the mortuary where the body lay. There the corpse was uncovered to reveal a beautiful young girl with a bullet wound right in the middle of her healthy bronzed body.

'Nothing much to help you there,' the pathologist said. 'The bullet went straight through her body.'

'From the front or back?' McLean asked.

'From the front, I think, but one can't be too sure about that. One thing is certain – death was almost instantaneous. She wouldn't have been able to swim a yard after being hit.'

'How far from land was she when it happened?' McLean asked the local police officer.

'Four to five hundred yards. We have the evidence of a man – an ex-army officer named Major Munroe who actually saw the thing happen from his bedroom window at the Radcliffe Hotel. He had his binoculars focused on the girl, and saw her struggling in the sea for a few moments.'

'Did he give you the actual time when it happened?'

'Yes. It was 7.35 in the morning. That time has been confirmed by the two men in the speedboat to which her tow-line was fastened. Probably your best witness is the film which was being taken. It was in colour and has not yet been processed, but we expect to get it some time this afternoon.'

McLean then took over the car, and after dropping the local officer at his headquarters he and Brook drove to the house where the dead girl's party were staying.

II

It was an immaculate building, standing in several acres of wooded grounds on a promontory in the wide waterway. At the lower part of the grounds was a curving stone wall which formed an anchorage for small craft, and floating in it was a red and blue raking-looking cabin cruiser. On ringing the door-bell a middle-aged man in

51

very abbreviated canvas shorts appeared.

'I am a police officer from London,' McLean told him. 'Are you related to the young woman who was drowned yesterday?'

'Yes. I was told the case had gone to London. Please come in. I am Edward Banting, cousin of Laura.'

He led them to a lounge which was wide open on the seaward side, and in which three other persons were sitting, drinking coffee. One of these was a rather faded blonde of uncertain age.

'My sister,' Banting said. 'Cecily, these gentlemen are from London, investigating poor Laura's death.'

The woman gave McLean a nod, and then dabbed her moist eyes with a tiny handkerchief.

'These two gentlemen represent the Acme Film Company,' Banting continued – 'Harry James and George Stillwell. Harry drives the speedboat and George takes the pictures.'

'Is this a private venture or commercial?' McLean asked.

'A bit of each,' Banting said. 'My cousin Laura had entered for a water-ski-ing competition which is to be held at the Lido at Venice in a fortnight's time. She was absolutely expert and I was successful in getting the film company interested in the making of a documentary. We looked around for a suitable place to take the film, and were lucky to find this quiet spot for the work.'

'At the time when Miss Banting fell into the sea did you hear any sound of a gun being fired?' McLean asked the lean photographer.

'Goodness, no! When the boat engine is on full throttle you can't hear yourself speak. We were doing nearly forty knots. I thought she had lost her balance. It took some time to get the speedboat round again, and I was amazed that she was not swimming. When – when we found her we discovered the ghastly reason.'

'Were there any boats in the vicinity?' McLean asked.

'Nothing within a mile. Not far from here there was a party fishing, but that's a long way from where we were operating.'

'Tell me more about your cousin,' McLean said. 'Does she normally live with her parents?'

'She had no parents. She was twenty years of age, and her father died a year ago. Her mother died some five years earlier. She sold the big family house, and bought a luxury flat in Baron's Court, Weybridge. My sister and I share a house in London.'

'Did she inherit much from her father?'

'Yes – quite a lot of property. Probate hasn't been obtained yet, but she must be worth close on a hundred thousand pounds.'

'Was she engaged in any kind of profession?'

'No.'

'Nor involved in any kind of love affair?'

'Not to my knowledge.'

'I'm not so sure about that,' Cecily said. 'I stayed with her for a few weeks after her father's death, and she had a number of telephone calls which she was very shy about. It was always a man, and I teased her a bit about it. She called him "Nick" and sometimes was very angry with him. I know no more than that.'

'Did she inherit her father's estate at once or were there any restrictions?'

'None at all. With the exception of legacies to myself and my brother the residue was to go to her absolutely.'

'Was she being paid by the Film Company for her work?'

'Yes. She was to get a thousand pounds when the film was finished.'

McLean then decided to see the one known independent witness of the tragedy – Major Munroe, and he found him sunning himself in the garden of the hotel.

'I'm sorry to bother you, sir,' he said. 'I know you have made a statement concerning what you witnessed yesterday from your bedroom window, but I should like a few more details.'

'Certainly. Fire away.'

'Is this the view you get from your bedroom?'

'Yes.'

'And you have estimated that the girl was about five hundred yards away when she went into the sea?'

'Yes.'

'What course was the boat on when it happened?'

'She was coming dead at me. I could just see the girl to the left of the man with the camera. When she went overboard the boat came round in a wide turn and went back to the spot where she had fallen. It seemed to cruise around for some time before they found her.'

'Did you hear any sound which might have been a rifle shot?'

'No. Only the high note of the engine.'

McLean was puzzled by the whole business, for the nearest land to the spot where the girl had fallen, with the exception of the hotel, was at least six hundred yards distant. It seemed incredible that any marksman could hit a comparatively small target at that distance, even with a telescopic sight.

'Could it have been an accident?' Brook asked. 'Some fool playing about with a rifle?'

'It could – a chance in a million. But if it wasn't that million to one chance there is only one set of circumstances which would make it possible.'

'And what are they?' Brook asked.

'It required that someone knew the time and place where the practice was usually done. I don't think that any Bisley expert would hope to hit a figure moving at forty miles an hour at five or six hundred yards range, unless the target was coming directly towards him. Then he would be able to fix it in his sights. But let's get back to head-quarters, to see if that film is available.'

III

McLean had to wait some time before the

film arrived. It was projected on a reduced screen in the laboratory, and McLean was able to observe the superb display given by the ski-girl.

'Any moment now,' the cameraman said, towards the end of the reel.

'Can you hold it?' McLean asked.

'Yes, for a moment or two.'

Then came the drama. McLean saw her release her grip on the tow-rope and screw up her face in agony.

'Hold it!' he said.

The film ceased to roll and McLean saw behind the girl a wide expanse of open water, but a painted buoy in the distance gave him his bearing.

'She wasn't shot from that direction,' he said. 'We are getting the point of view we got from the hotel garden, but a little more to the right. It means that the shot was fired from some place behind the hotel, from high ground, I think, as the bullet appeared to have travelled through the girl's body at a downward angle. We'll act on that clue at once.'

Later they parked their car at the hotel, and then walked through the semi-tropical grounds at the rear of the building. It led them to a well-made road which served the hotel, but to the right McLean found a rough track which appeared to lead to the higher land. For a time the bulk of the hotel blocked any seaward view but as they climbed higher the whole lovely estuary came in sight.

'There's the buoy!' McLean said. 'But we have to go to the right a bit to get it in line with that distant church spire.'

A little further on, in a slight depression which had held recent rain, they found tyre impressions in the moist soil and McLean stopped and made a rough sketch of the pattern of the tread.

'Not British,' he said. 'They look like an American type.'

'There's an old ruin away to the right,' Brook said. 'Look through those trees.'

McLean nodded and pushed on. He saw no further tyre tracks but now the road seemed to lead to the old ruin which was more clearly visible, and a minute or two later they stood outside a ruined building in a small clearing. Close to it was a deep pit surrounded by a broken-down wire fence.

'An old tin mine,' McLean said. 'More tyre tracks too. They come to a dead end. A car must have stood here for some time. This looks promising.'

They entered the doorless building, but a tree interfered with the clear seaward view. McLean went up the rickety staircase which looked like falling down at any moment. In the upper room he got an absolutely clear view of the estuary. There was the buoy almost dead in line with the distant church spire, exactly as he had seen it in the film. On the floor the grime of ages was disturbed by recent footprints.

'A man with rubber soles,' he said. 'Get the camera from the car, Brook, while I measure up these impressions.'

When Brook returned he found McLean examining a half-burnt cheroot, and two used matches of the strip type.

'The marksman waited and smoked until the speedboat appeared and then stubbed out the cheroot with his foot,' McLean said. 'There's a mark on the window ledge where he rested his gun. A short time ago we met a man who was smoking a cheroot. Remember?'

'I can't recall that,' Brook admitted.

'Your memory needs brushing up. It was Banting. While he spoke to us it was between his fingers. All this adds up, doesn't it?'

Brook had to admit that it did, but added

that he failed to see why Banting should want to kill his own cousin who he seemed keen to make famous.

'I can, provided she died intestate. He and his sister would then be next of kin, with a hundred thousand pounds in the kitty. I can't see a young woman in perfect health making a will. But take that photograph and then we'll get back to headquarters.'

When they were on firm ground McLean noticed some faint footmarks going towards the piled earth on the side of the pit. He followed them as far as they went, and then came back, very reflective.

'Stay here, Brook,' he said. 'I'm going to get some men and a rope.'

McLean was back in an hour with three hefty men and a long coil of rope, and electric torches. Two of the men hung on the rope while the third was lowered into the pit. A second coil had to be added before a shout came up from the depths, and the rope suddenly slacked.

'Okay!' the voice bellowed. 'There's no water, and I've found a gun.'

'Hold it by the barrel,' McLean called. 'Ready now?'

'Yes.'

The man was hauled to the surface, and

McLean caught it by the barrel and relieved him of it. It was a service rifle, and clamped to it was a telescopic sight, broken at the rear. In the magazine were six cartridges, and the dial sight registered six hundred yards. The precious exhibit was taken to police headquarters and handed over to the fingerprint men. For hours the fingerprint men worked on the weapon, and when at last they produced good prints of fingers near the butt McLean was awakened from sleep at his hotel and told the glad news.

Early the next morning McLean and Brook went to 'Tideways'. In the unlocked garage they found two cars. One was a two-seater sports car and the other a large American saloon. The tyres on the latter corresponded with the impression which McLean had found near the old mine.

'Now we'll go inside,' McLean said.

When McLean rang the bell it was Banting who came to the door. He looked quite unperturbed and gave them a greeting.

'Sorry to trouble you,' McLean said. 'But can I have a word with you?'

'Of course. Please come in.'

He led them into the sun-lounge where the two film men were having breakfast.

'Don't let me interrupt you,' McLean said. 'But whose saloon car is that in the garage?'

'Ours,' said the tall cameraman.

'Has it been garaged here all the time?'

'Yes.'

'Was it here when you went out in the speedboat with Laura Banting?'

'Yes.'

'And also when you got back from that ill-fated trip?'

'Yes.'

'Was it possible for anyone to use the car during your absence?'

'Yes. The ignition key hadn't been removed.'

McLean then asked to see Banting's sister, but was told she was still in bed. At his request she was brought downstairs and McLean saw her in another room.

'Do you always sleep late?' he asked.

'Yes, I'm afraid I do.'

'Did you sleep late on the morning before yesterday?'

'Not very late. I never eat breakfast. Usually I come downstairs round about ten o'clock, but on that day my brother came and woke me up and told me the bad news about Laura.'

'At about what time?'

'I can't remember exactly. I think it must have been round about nine o'clock.'

'And you were sound asleep until then?'

'Yes.'

'Did your brother ever keep a rifle?' McLean asked.

This very significant question caused her breast to heave and her eyes to become full of terror.

'Year – years ago,' she stammered, 'but I think he got rid of it.'

Now McLean's mind was made up. He rejoined the man in the other room.

'Mr Banting,' he said. 'I should like you to come with us to police headquarters, to have your fingerprints taken.'

Banting stared at him and for the first time he showed disquiet.

'This is purely routine,' McLean added.

'I – I understand.'

He was taken away a few minutes later, and upon arrival at police headquarters his fingerprints were taken. They proved to be identical with those on the butt of the deadly weapon. He was detained and on the following morning was charged. He pleaded 'not guilty' but by then McLean had the rubber-soled shoes which he had worn, and the issue was never in doubt.

4

Old Gold

I

Peter Duncan, home on leave from his archaeological post in the Middle East heard the telephone ringing while having his breakfast at his widowed mother's house in the country, not far from Horsham. He was about to answer it when he heard his mother's voice taking the call. She entered the dining-room a few moments later.

'There's a man wanting to speak to you, Peter,' she said. 'He says his name is Ronald Patterson.'

'Good gracious!' ejaculated Peter. 'I had no idea he was in England.'

He hurried to the telephone, had a fairly long conversation and then returned to the dining-room where his mother was now seated.

'He arrived in London only yesterday,' he said. 'Wants to come and see me. I told him

I should be glad to see him, and have invited him to lunch. Will that be all right?'

'Of course. Is he coming by train?'

'No, he has hired a car for a week or two, and will come by road. I think you must remember him, Mother. He came here when I was last home on leave. A very tall chap, fair haired and with a slight stammer.'

'Yes, of course, but I had forgotten his name.'

'Seems to be doing quite well for he is staying at the Savoy.'

'You'd better get some drink in,' Mrs Duncan said. 'We are very short of it.'

'I'll run into the town presently. I'd like to know what he has been doing. The last time I saw him he was travelling around making documentary films.'

Later Peter drove into the town and bought some drink, since he intended to invite Patterson to spend the night with them. Mrs Duncan laid the table for three, embellishing it with fresh flowers from the garden and by half past twelve all was ready for their guest.

But at one o'clock Patterson had not arrived, and at half past the hour the situation was the same. Mrs Duncan was very upset for it meant that the nice meal she had planned was going to be spoiled.

'It looks as if he has had some trouble on the road,' Peter said. 'But it's strange that he hasn't telephoned to say he has been delayed.'

At two o'clock they were compelled to start their meal, and after they had finished Peter decided to telephone the hotel to find out if possible what time Patterson had left. After some delay he was told that Patterson had left at eleven o'clock in a hire car which had been left for him at the hotel. The number was not known but the hall porter had stated that it was a blue Alvis saloon.

The Duncans waited in vain all that day, and in the evening Peter rang the hotel again and was told that Patterson had not shown up there.

'That's very queer,' Peter said. 'I think I ought to go to the police. Patterson was a bit mysterious on the telephone. He said he had something very important to show me. If he did have an accident on the road he may have been taken to some hospital.'

'But wouldn't the police have communicated with the hotel? They could trace him by the car registration.'

'Yes, but they may not have had time yet, especially with a hire firm involved. I think

I'll run into town and tell the police.'

At the police station the sergeant at the reception desk wrote down the complaint, and Peter was kept quite a long time while the telephone was used and the accident lists consulted. Finally he was told that there had been no accident in which an Alvis car was involved, and he went back home a little relieved, but greatly puzzled.

It was on the following morning while he and his mother were having breakfast that there came a ring on the doorbell, and a few moments later the daily help entered the room to inform them that two police officers from London had called and were asking to see Mr Peter Duncan.

'Show them into the sitting-room, Mary,' Peter said. 'I'll come in a few moments.'

'It must be about your friend,' Mrs Duncan said. 'Oh dear, I hope it isn't bad news.'

Peter shook his head in a perplexed way, and then drank his coffee and went to the sitting-room. The taller of the two plain-clothed officers turned from the bookcase in which he appeared to be interested.

'I hope I haven't disturbed you, Mr Duncan,' he said.

'Not at all,' Peter said. 'Is it about my old

friend Ronald Patterson?'

'Yes, I am Inspector McLean from Scotland Yard, and this is Sergeant Brook. Your enquiry at the local police station came through to us last night, and early this morning there were developments. A blue Alvis saloon was found abandoned not far from Wisley on the London road. In your statement to the county police you said that Patterson was staying at the Savoy. We have already called there and I have here a passport which was found in his bedroom. You might look at the photograph and tell me if it is the man you were expecting.'

Peter took the passport and saw the unmistakable face of Patterson.

'That's the man,' he said.

'What can you tell us about him?'

'I've know him for about fifteen years. He was rather an adventurous chap – and quite unpredictable. We were at the same public school, but we parted when I went up to Cambridge. I saw him again years afterwards. He was then employed in some film company, but later after his father had died and left him some money he gave up film work and started on his own making travel films which he sold mainly in the United States. Some time afterwards he turned up at the place where I am employed in archaeological work in the Middle East, and took some film there. The following year he called here, knowing I was on leave. That was three years ago. I haven't seen him since.'

'Was his projected call here yesterday merely social?'

'Mainly, I suppose, but on the telephone he said he had something very interesting to show me.'

'Did he give you any idea what it was?'

'No, but he said it was up my street, and that I might be able to give him some advice.'

'Do you know anything about his family?'

'He had no family after the death of his father.'

McLean finally thanked Peter, and then went back to the police car with Brook.

'It doesn't get us much further,' he said. 'But I should like to know what it was that he wanted to show Duncan. Now let's have a look at the spot where the car was found.'

II

After about half an hour's run they found

the spot. It was clearly marked on the large-scale map, a hundred yards or so from the main road to London, and behind a clump of silver birch trees which fringed the woodland. Away to the left was a small shallow pond which McLean knew had been searched. Near the site were some pieces of paper, and the ashes of an old fire left by untidy campers. The tracks of the car were still visible up to the spot where it had finally rested.

'Gather up all those bits of paper and that bottle,' McLean said to Brook. 'They look too old to be of any use as evidence, but at least we can leave the place tidy.'

While Brook was thus engaged, McLean examined very carefully the ground around the site, and between the site and the main road. He found nothing of any interest at all and returned to Brook who had gathered quite a considerable quantity of litter in a cardboard box.

'No luck,' he told Brook. 'I'll look through that litter in the car. Now we'll go and have a look at that Alvis and hear what the fingerprint men have to say.'

They walked back to the police car, and while Brook was driving McLean went through the filthy litter. Most of it was very old, and partly scorched. The bottle was older still, but a crunched cigarette packet was comparatively clean. He twisted it into its original shape, and saw something scribbled across a plain portion.

'A telephone number,' he said. 'Not very plain – but it looks like "Tem. 26723 or 25" underneath is "Pretty P. 5. 2.w".'

'A telephoned bet to a bookie,' Brook said.

'It looks like it. We'll check up that number later.'

When they reached county police head-quarters McLean was informed that the car had yielded several lots of fingerprints, and all from the same hands.

'Probably the owner's,' the fingerprint expert said. 'For some of them date back quite a long time. There were none at all on the steering wheel where we expected to find them. I don't think these are going to be much help to you.'

McLean was of the same opinion when he saw the car and the places from which the fingerprints had been taken.

'There's little doubt that Patterson was followed from his hotel and held up on his way to Horsham,' he said. 'It may not have been anywhere near the place where the car was found. The persons responsible had the sense to keep the steering wheel clean. Now find out who owns that Temple Bar telephone number.'

Brook was soon back with the required information.

'It's a bookmaker named Passmore in King Street,' he said. 'I know the man. He's not in business in a big way.'

'We'll see him now,' McLean said.

A few minutes later they found Passmore's office on the second floor. McLean asked to see the head of the firm, and he and Brook were shown into an office where a large bald-headed man was sitting at a desk.

'What can I do with you, Inspector?' he asked.

'I'm looking for a man who placed a bet with you recently. I don't know his name, but the bet was on a dog or horse named Pretty something or other. The bet was five pounds each way.'

'I don't recall the bet, but there was a horse named Pretty Polly which ran at Sandown Park a few days ago. It didn't even get a place.'

'That may well be the animal,' McLean said. 'Can you tell me who the backer was?'

'Yes. I'll find out.'

He pushed a bell button and a young clerk

entered the room. Passmore asked him to bring the betting records for the race in question, and a minute or two later he returned with a huge book and handed it to Passmore who opened it at a page indicated by a slip of paper.

'I had a dozen bets on that horse,' he said. 'It was well fancied but failed to get anywhere. Ah, here's the entry. The only one for the amount you mentioned. The backer was Philip Rushton of No. 10 Chaucer House, Kensington.'

'Has he had an account here long?' McLean asked.

'Only about six months. He was recommended by another client, but doesn't bet very often.'

'Who was the other client?'

'A Mr Bland, Torton Lodge, Parson's Lane, Wimbledon. He's a very old client of mine.'

'Have you ever met Rushton?' McLean asked.

'No.'

'Nor Bland?'

'Yes. I used to live almost next door to him. He travels abroad a great deal. I think he has some kind of business in Egypt or thereabouts.'

McLean thanked him and then he and Brook drove on to Chaucer House.

They found Rushton at home. He was a well-built man of about thirty years of age, and invited them in when McLean told him that he might be able to help him in a certain investigation.

'Mr Rushton,' McLean said, 'do you know a bookmaker named Passmore in King's Street, Covent Garden?'

'Yes,' he said. 'I have a bet with him now and then, but I've never actually met him.'

'Did you have a bet with him recently, on a horse that ran at Sandown Park?'

'Yes, to my sorrow. I lost ten quid on it.'

'Was it tipped to you, or did you back it on form?'

'It was tipped. I met a friend of mine in a pub on the day of the race. He said it was a certainty, and I was fool enough to believe him. I had only about ten minutes to get the money on, so I used the pub telephone.'

McLean then produced the empty cigarette packet, and showed it to him.

'Did you discard that packet some time afterwards?' McLean asked.

'I must have done,' he said. 'For that is my handwriting. I wrote it on the packet because I had nothing else to write on. I had to look it up in the telephone directory because I couldn't remember the bookmaker's address. Where did you find it?'

'In a wood off the London road to Horsham. Does that help you?'

'Yes, it does. I had to go to Guildford on the day after the race. It was a gorgeous day and I had had a heavy lunch. I drove the car off the road and had a nap in it at a quiet place near a lake. I remember now that I smoked my last cigarette there and must have thrown the empty packet through the window.'

'You are sure it was the day after the race?' McLean asked.

'Quite sure.'

'Well, thank you very much,' McLean said. 'I'm sorry to have troubled you.'

'Not at all,' Rushton said.

III

'What do you make of that, Inspector?' Brook asked when they were back in the car.

'I make him out to be a liar,' McLean said. 'Of course he had to admit that the cigarette packet was his, but that race took place four days before the Alvis car was dumped, and

I'll never believe that the packet lay where we found it for three whole days for we have had continuous rain for two of those days. Why is the packet bone-dry?'

'That's a point,' Brook said. 'But what do we do about it?'

'I'm going to presume that this is a clear case of kidnapping and to get a warrant to remove Patterson's baggage from his hotel and examine it carefully.'

Some hours later McLean carried out this plan, and removed two normal-sized suit-cases, and a very heavy one. They all bore many hotel labels from cities in the Middle East. The two smaller ones were easily opened, and contained chiefly clothing and some souvenirs. But the heavy case was locked and, in the absence of a key, had to be forced. Inside was a cine-camera, and several reels of film marked 'exposed', together with a lot of smaller gadgets connected with photography.

'We'll have a film show all on our own,' McLean said. 'I'll lay that on now.'

Later, in a private studio, they sat and watched the film being reeled off. The pictures were mainly of ancient cities and desert wastes, all very clear and artistically done. Then suddenly the photographer switched to subjects less remote, and showed the grounds of a hotel on the banks of a great river.

'The Nile, I think,' McLean said. 'That's the great pyramid of Cheops in the background.'

The camera again switched to the interior of a wide veranda, with a group of men drinking at a table.

'Hold it!' McLean said to the man in charge of the projector.

The film ceased to revolve.

'Look at the man close to the potted plant,' McLean said to Brook.

'My hat!' Brook ejaculated. 'It's Rushton!'

The rest of the film was reeled off but the group was not seen again.

'Mr Rushton has a lot to explain,' McLean said. 'What was he doing out there with Patterson? I think we've got him on a hook.'

'But not landed,' Brook said. 'Do we go and see him again?'

'Not at once. I want to see the man who introduced him to that bookmaker. He should be able to give us some information about Rushton. Get me down to Wimbledon.'

Mr Bland's house at Wimbledon was very close to the Common. It was very old and set in a nice garden of about an acre. Brook drove the car close to the front door, and when McLean rang the bell the door was opened by a powerfully built middle-aged man. In a moment McLean recognised him as one of the men in the group he had seen in the film. Brook gave McLean a quick glance for he too remembered that bull-headed fellow.

'Mr Bland?' McLean asked.

'Yes.'

'I am a police officer, and should like to have a few words with you about a man of your acquaintance.'

'Better come in,' Bland said, and showed them into a reception room, with wide windows looking on to the terrace and garden.

'I believe you know a man named Philip Rushton.'

'Yes. I've known him for a couple of years.'

'Have you seen him recently?'

'No. Not for some weeks, I think he's abroad.'

'Do you know a man named Patterson, who makes documentary films?'

'No – I can't say I do. What is he like?'

'You should know perfectly well,' McLean said. 'For he took some close-up film of you and your friend Rushton in a hotel along the Nile quite recently.'

'You must be mistaken,' Bland protested. 'If he took those photographs it must have been a long time ago, and without my knowledge. What does all this...'

He stopped as through the wide window he saw a car arrive outside and Rushton himself step out of it. Rushton took one look at the police car, and hesitated for a moment.

'Get him, Brook,' McLean said. 'You'll have to be quick.'

Brook was quick enough to prevent Rushton getting back into his own car, and a few moments later he came into the room, with Rushton looking very hangdog.

'Sit down, Mr Rushton,' McLean said. 'I've a few questions to ask you.'

But before McLean could put his questions there came the sound from above of smashing glass, and Bland winced as if he had been struck.

'Stay here, Brook,' McLean said. 'I'm going up.'

McLean mounted the stairs two at a time, peered into the rooms on the first floor, and then mounted to the floor above. Here he found a locked door, but the key was on the outside. He entered the room to find a man in a precarious position on a platform of chairs built up on a bed under a skylight. The floor beneath was littered with broken glass, and the man striving to climb out on to the roof.

'Come down, Mr Patterson,' he called. 'I am a police officer.'

The young man descended, and stood for a moment breathing heavily from his exertions.

'I presume you are Mr Patterson?' McLean asked.

'Yes. I was followed from my hotel and kidnapped.'

'Why?' McLean asked.

'I – I don't know.'

'I think you do know,' McLean replied. 'But come downstairs and we'll sort that out.'

In the downstairs room when Patterson came face to face with his two associates he had a change of mind.

'I'll tell you the truth, Inspector,' he said. 'On that last trip of mine, to take some film somewhere near the boundaries of Libya and Egypt, Bland and Rushton were with me. While investigating an old cave I made an interesting discovery. It was an ancient broken jar, and in the bottom of it were some gold coins. I knew they were valuable and that I should have handed them over to the responsible authority, but I was persuaded by Rushton not to be a fool especially as we didn't know which country owned the spot where they were found. Back in Cairo we talked the matter over, and decided to keep our mouths shut, and to share the proceeds – one half to me and the other half between my companions. But later I had second thoughts. I left the next night by taxi and was fortunate in catching a boat from Alexandria. When I got home I got in touch with an old friend of mine – Peter Duncan – who is an expert archaeologist, and planned to take one of the coins to him to get his opinion of its value. I didn't know that Bland and Rushton had beaten me by using a plane. They hijacked me, and took the coin from my pocket. Rushton now has it. They wanted to know what I had done with the bulk, and threatened to hold me until I told them. That's the whole story.'

McLean held out his hand to the frustrated Rushton.

'The coin,' he said.

Rushton hesitated for a moment and then

produced the ancient gold coin. It was in perfect condition although somewhat tarnished.

'How many others were there?' he asked Patterson.

'Thirty-one.'

'And what did you do with them?'

'I handed them to my bank for safe keeping.'

Bland and Rushton were taken into custody, and Patterson told to return to his hotel and stay there until McLean saw him again.

Later in the day McLean paid a visit to Peter Duncan, and showed him the gold coin. He opened his eyes with astonishment.

'Where on earth did you get this?' he asked.

'It's what your friend was coming to see you about when he was kidnapped. He came upon a hoard of them in the Middle East while making a film.'

'It's an Egyptian octadrachm of two centuries B.C.' Duncan said. 'It's worth at least £300. He always was a lucky devil, but he should have handed them over to the proper authority.'

'He knew that, but was tempted and fell

from grace. He is now back in his hotel. His two associates who followed him from Egypt and who kidnapped him are not so comfortably lodged. Don't try to see him, but there is no harm in your ringing him, and hearing his doleful story. You might advise him to get a good lawyer.'

5

Mrs Rignold's Guest

I

Mrs Rignold's Guest House in Bloomsbury had an unblemished reputation in that area, for Mrs Rignold was most selective in her boarders, all of whom were women and whom she invariably referred to as 'my young ladies'. No men callers were allowed, and if any of the boarders wanted to stay out after 11 p.m. they had to provide good reason for so doing.

Inspector McLean knew Mrs Rignold quite well, for in the past he had been successful in tracking down a burglar who had broken into her house and got away with some booty. He was surprised one morning at the office to be told that Mrs Rignold was in the waiting-room, requesting to see him in person on a matter of considerable importance.

'I'll see her,' he said. 'I hope she hasn't been burgled again.'

A minute or two later Mrs Rignold entered the office. She was bulky and out of breath, and Sergeant Brook swiftly provided her with a chair.

'It's good of you, Inspector,' she panted. 'I know I shouldn't have asked for you in person, but...'

'That's quite all right,' McLean assured her. 'Now, what's the trouble?'

'It's one of my young ladies – a very nice girl named Hedda Larsen. She's Swedish and comes from a very respectable family in Stockholm. She went out last night at about eight o'clock and hasn't returned. I'm sure something has happened to her because she is such a quiet, well-behaved girl. I'm certain she wouldn't leave me to worry like this if she were able to get in touch with me.'

'How long has she been staying with you?' McLean asked.

'Five months. Her mother brought her over

here after I had had some correspondence with her. She was recommended to me by another Swedish girl who stayed with me years ago.'

'What is she doing in London?'

'She is a student at the University. She speaks English very well and is taking a course in Economics, I think. Oh, I remembered to bring a photograph of her which her mother sent me before I actually saw her.'

She delved into her handbag and produced a snapshot of a dark, very attractive young girl, smiling rather roguishly at the camera.

'She would be about a year older now,' she explained. 'But this is exactly like her.'

'Did you see her leave your house last night?' McLean asked.

'Yes. She told me she was going to see a travel film, but didn't say where. All she had with her was a red morocco handbag. But now I must tell you something. A minute or two after Hedda had left another boarder – Edith Knowle – came in. This morning, when I was making enquiries, Miss Knowle told me that she is almost certain that she saw Hedda get into a saloon car which had been waiting near the house. The driver got out to open the door for her. He appeared to be fairly young and very tall. They drove off in the other direction.'

'Had she a regular boy-friend?' McLean asked.

'No. I'm sure she hadn't. She was very studious and spent most of her evenings in her room. If she did go out in the evening she always came home very early.'

It looked very much like a storm in a tea-cup, and McLean pointed out that it was far too early to assume that anything tragic had happened to the missing girl, but he promised to make enquiries to see if the girl had perhaps been involved in some accident and taken to hospital.

'I'll keep in touch with you, Mrs Rignold,' he said. 'If the girl should come back, please let me know at once.'

McLean made his enquiries but failed to find any victim of street accidents who might conceivably be the missing girl, and during that day there was no further word from Mrs Rignold. But early the next morning McLean called on Mrs Rignold to find out if there was any change in the situation.

'Oh, I'm so glad you called, Inspector,' said Mrs Rignold. 'I've just had a telephone message from Hedda. She said she was quite all right, and sorry if she had caused me any alarm. She hopes to be back tomorrow when she will explain everything.'

McLean wrinkled his brow at this quite unexpected happening.

'Did she give you no idea where she was speaking from?' he asked.

'No. I asked her that, but she repeated that she would explain everything when she saw me.'

'Can you be sure that it was Hedda who was speaking?' McLean asked.

'Oh yes. Her voice was quite clear and I recognised her queer little accent.'

'Was it a long-distance call?'

'It couldn't have been because when I picked up the receiver I spoke directly to her.'

'Did she ask if you had notified the police?'

'She said that if I had notified the police I had better tell them that everything was all right. I said I would do that and then she rang off.'

McLean was reflective for a few moments and Mrs Rignold, watching his face, knew that he was far from satisfied.

'You – you don't trust that telephone call?'

she asked.

'No. When that girl left this house she obviously had no intention of staying away for even one night, since she took nothing with her except a handbag. I should like to take up that question of the waiting car mentioned by Miss Knowle. Does she happen to be in the house?'

'Yes, I think she is just about to go to business. I'll bring her down here.'

She left and returned with Miss Knowle a few minutes later. Miss Knowle was round about twenty-five, rather plain but very intelligent.

'Miss Knowle,' said McLean. 'You told Mrs Rignold that you thought you saw Hedda Larsen enter a waiting car just after she left this house two nights ago. Can you be a little more explicit?'

'I could have been mistaken,' said Miss Knowle. 'As I never actually saw her face. But I did recognise her clothes, and the red handbag, also her walk. She wiggles a bit – like Marilyn what's her name, and when I saw her she was between the house and the waiting car. Mrs Rignold agrees about the clothes.'

'That's right,' said Mrs Rignold. 'A grey suit, suede shoes and a tiny grey felt hat.'

'Did you notice the make of car?' McLean asked Miss Knowle.

'It was a low-built sports saloon – ivory shade. I was not close enough to read the number plate.'

'Tell me about the man who was driving. You said he was very tall and young. Anything outstanding about him?'

'Curly fair hair. He wore no hat when I saw him. Quite a handsome athletic type.'

In reply to further questions Miss Knowle said that her impression had been that Hedda had no interest at all in young men, but was entirely immersed in her studies.

II

When Miss Knowle had left McLean found himself in a quandary, and he unburdened himself to Mrs Rignold.

'I have no authority to search Miss Larsen's room,' he said. 'To get it would involve delay, especially in view of that telephone call. I am convinced it was intended to cause delay at this end. I think that in the circumstances you are justified in searching Miss Larsen's room. There might be information there which would help this investigation. What do you say?'

Mrs Rignold was nothing if not co-operative, and she nodded her head and swiftly produced a duplicate key to Hedda's bedroom. McLean went with her up the stairs and they entered the room together. It was scrupulously clean and tidy, and in a bookcase by the bed were a number of textbooks on Economics. Some nice articles of toilet were laid out neatly on the dressing-table and at the rear was a small framed photograph of a young man. McLean picked it up.

'Has she a brother?' he asked Mrs Rignold.

'No.'

'Then this could be the man mentioned by Miss Knowle. There's the fair curly hair, and the athletic build. Look for correspondence. There may be some communication from him.'

There were letters, but none from a man. Then to McLean's great joy a small diary was brought to light. In it there was not a single reference to any man, but tucked between the pages there was a rather bad snapshot of Hedda Larsen standing beside a sports saloon car, and the registration number of the car was perfectly clear.

'I want the two photographs, but not the diary,' McLean said. 'Thank you, Mrs Rignold.'

On his way back to Scotland Yard McLean called at the bank where Miss Knowle was employed and saw her privately. She recognised both the man and the car, and McLean went on his way feeling that something had been achieved.

'News from the Larsen girl,' he said to Sergeant Brook. 'Her landlady received a telephone message this morning telling her that the girl is all right and that we need bother no more in the matter.'

'What was it – an elopement?' Brook asked.

'No, Brook. The girl is being held for some reason. Here's the man she went away with, and this is the car he used. I want the owner traced without delay.'

'You mean the telephone message was a fake?'

'It must have been. But get on to the registration authority and find the present owner of the car.'

It did not take Brook very long to get the information required and he came back to McLean and read out the details.

'Jaguar 2.4 Sports Saloon. Purchased by a

Major Williams two years ago, transferred to Peter Lockwood, Postgate Lodge, Esher, four months ago. Colour ivory white.'

'He's our man,' said McLean. 'There's a lot he will have to explain. Let's get going.'

A few minutes later they were on the road in a fast car and half an hour later they were in the pleasant little town. Here McLean got the exact location of Postgate Lodge from the police station. It was a rather isolated lodge of an old country house which had completely disappeared. Brook pulled up the car outside the small habitation. A garage had recently been added, but the door of this was open, and it was seen to be empty.

'Looks as if there is nobody at home,' said Brook. 'There's a couple of milk bottles outside the back door.'

They left the car and walked up the short drive to the front door. McLean pushed the bell button, and heard the bell ringing inside, but there was no response. He then tried the door handle, and to his surprise the door opened. He then called 'Anyone at home?' in a loud voice, but all was silent. He was hesitating whether to enter when suddenly he saw a dark patch on the rug just inside the door. He went forward and touched it with his fingers. They came away coloured a deep red.

'Blood!' he ejaculated. 'Well, now we will go in.'

The room on the right was a shambles. There was more blood on the floor and a table had been overturned. Drawers had been ransacked and left open. On a low table near the fireplace with a half-bottle of sherry, and two wine glasses. One of the glasses had lipstick on the brim.

'The girl?' asked Brook, as he noticed this.

'Quite likely, and somebody was badly injured. Look, he lay on that couch for a bit. Plenty of blood there.'

The other rooms were similarly dis-arranged, and in the bathroom a small hanging cupboard had been left open. It was full of medical articles including some bandages.

'That tells part of the story,' McLean said. 'The injured person was bleeding badly and needed bandaging. My guess is that Lockwood brought the girl here in his car. They had some drinks and then the place was entered by other persons and a fight took place. The intruders were looking for something, and I don't think they were successful.'

93

'Why not?' Brook asked.

'Because of the absence of Lockwood's car. I think they used Lockwood's car to take him and the girl away. Nothing else makes any sense. Now get me through to the Yard. I want that car traced – and quickly.'

III

That evening McLean and Sergeant Brook sat by the telephone waiting for any possible response to the earlier police broadcast, or news from the cottage near Esher where McLean had posted two men with orders to detain any persons who might arrive there. It was clear to Sergeant Brook that McLean was worried by the dead-end at which they had arrived. He had been on the telephone to Mrs Rignold who had tearfully reported no change in the situation.

'I still don't quite understand why the girl and Lockwood were taken away,' Brook said.

'I think I do,' said McLean. 'She was a witness to what took place in that cottage. I think she's just an innocent little fool who fell for a handsome crook and kept it a dead secret. I believe Lockwood was in hiding from some friends of his whom he had double-crossed in the past. There's something which he has which they want badly. They are not likely to let the girl go until they have got what they want. If Lockwood is badly injured and should die on their hands we may never see the girl again. That's the situation as I see it, and I don't like it at all.'

Brook didn't like it either, for he foresaw more weary hours of vain waiting, but at seven o'clock the silence was broken as a telephone call was plugged through to McLean. He picked up the receiver and an excited voice came through so clearly that Brook could overhear every word.

'My name's Jim Brent,' it said. 'I've seen the Jaguar car mentioned in the police broadcast after the six o'clock news. I was in a pub at the time, sheltering from the rain. When the rain eased off I got on my bike again and cycled towards my home near Ripley. But after I had gone a few miles there was another terrific downpour and I had to take shelter. I saw a farm gate with a barn just inside it, so I nipped through and found the barn door ajar. When I got inside I saw a car parked there, covered by a tarpaulin. I lifted the back of the tarpaulin and saw the number plate. It fair took my breath away, for I remembered the number given in the broadcast. It's the car all right.'

'Where are you speaking from?' McLean asked.

'The telephone box on the junction of the London road with the lane that leads to Oxshott. It's two miles short of Cobham, on the left-hand side, and about a mile from the place where I saw the car.'

'Can you possibly wait there?' McLean asked. 'I could be with you in about half an hour.'

Brent agreed to do that and McLean replaced the receiver and got into action.

'I think it's genuine,' he said. 'In any case I can't afford to disregard it. Get a fast car, Brook, while I draw a couple of guns. We'll take Kennedy too in case of trouble.'

Brook's boredom had vanished at this prospect of action, and a few minutes later he and McLean and the extra man were in swift motion. They had little trouble in finding the telephone box, where a little drenched man with his cycle was waiting. The cycle was slung on the back of the big car and the informer sat with Kennedy in the back.

'Did you see the farmhouse?' McLean asked him.

'Yes. It lies away to the right of the barn. I didn't see anybody about.'

Very soon Brent signified that they were near the place and the car slowed down, and finally stopped at a five-barred gate.

'There's the barn,' said Brent.

'Good! You'd better stay here in the car.'

The three other men got out, and McLean and Brook went into the barn. There was the car without doubt. All the doors were locked, but McLean's torch, directed through a rear window, revealed that the floor carpet had been removed.

'Bloodstains, I imagine,' he said. 'Well, we'll see who is at home. Brook, here's your gun, but I hope we shan't need it. Kennedy, you'd better stay outside the door when we enter. Come on!'

They moved towards the front door of the poor-looking farmhouse, and a ring at the bell brought a sinister-looking man to the door. He scanned them furtively.

'Are you the owner of this property?' McLean asked.

'Yes. My name is Dyson.'

'We are police officers. I believe you have a Mr Lockwood here.'

'Lockwood? No, you are mistaken.'

'Then what is his car doing in your barn?'

This question was certainly unexpected for Dyson had no immediate reply.

'Oh – oh, that car,' he stammered. 'It was left there – by a man – after it had conked out, and–'

'I have reason to believe you are holding a man here,' McLean interrupted. 'Get into that room. I am going to search this house.'

Dyson turned his head towards the half-open door on the left, and then retreated towards it as Brook made a forward movement. Seated in the room was another man, with a bandaged head and a strip of plaster on his jaw.

'My – my brother,' stammered Dyson. 'Bill, they want to search the house. They're police…'

The seated man suddenly whipped out a pistol, but Brook was ready for that and uppercut him with a blow that sent him down with a crash. Within a few seconds he was handcuffed to his brother who offered no resistance. McLean picked up the fallen weapon.

'Look after them, Brook,' he said. 'I won't be long.'

In an upstairs room McLean found

Lockwood lying on a bed. There were bandages round his chest, and he looked like death. McLean spoke to him, and the eyes opened for a moment.

'Listen,' said McLean. 'I'm a police officer. Were you shot or stabbed?'

'Shot,' whispered Lockwood. 'Bill Dyson did it. We're all crooks – big robbery in Dublin six months ago. We quarrelled – afterwards – and I got away with the stuff. They tracked me down – thought I had most of it hidden, but I had sold it. I – I...'

He stopped as some blood trickled from his lips.

'Too ... late ... now,' he whispered. 'I'm dying. They tried to get the bullet out ... made things worse. That girl ... Hedda ... she knows nothing ... meant to go straight with her. She's up there.'

He pointed a shaking finger above him, and McLean went along the passage and found a narrow staircase leading to an attic. He opened the locked door and saw the pathetic figure of Hedda Larsen lying on a bed with her arms bound and a scarf tied round her mouth. Swiftly he cut the bonds and removed the scarf. Her terrified eyes stared up at him.

'It's all right,' he said. 'I am a police

officer. The two men responsible are in custody. Are you hurt?'

'Oh, thank God!' she said. 'No, I'm not hurt. They fed me and told me they would let me go when Mr Lockwood was better. They forced me to speak on the telephone to my landlady. But tell me about Mr Lockwood. Is he all right?'

'I'm afraid Mr Lockwood is beyond human aid,' McLean said. 'I will get a doctor here immediately, but I don't think there is any hope.'

Tears welled up in her eyes.

'Can – can I see him?' she asked.

'If you are able to walk.'

'I can – I can.'

He helped her rise to her feet, and after a few moments she made a few steps. Then he helped her down the stairs and finally they entered the room where Lockwood lay. But they were too late for Lockwood had ceased to breathe. A great sob escaped her, and McLean held her for a few moments.

'Don't fret too much,' he said. 'He was a self-confessed crook and you are well rid of him. But his two late partners will get their desserts. I have now to get a police van. After that I will take you home.'

6

A Cornish Holiday

I

Inspector McLean was not really enjoying his annual holiday at Corby Cove in South Cornwall. He had been much attracted to the place in the early spring, when he had stayed at the Beach Hotel for a couple of nights, and being told that it was usually booked up by the time summer came round, he booked himself a rather nice room, overlooking half a mile of lovely sand over which the Atlantic rollers roared in at every tide.

But, alas, the promise of spring was not borne out in August when he arrived, for the hotel was bursting at the seams, with a most curious lot of people, mostly young and rumbustious, and the noise of transistors, inside the hotel and outside, was nerve-racking.

'This is a bit disappointing,' McLean said

to a serious-minded fellow guest named Mayhew. 'When I booked up in the spring it wasn't a bit like this.'

'There's a reason,' Mayhew said. 'The head waiter told me that half these people came as a block booking. They're from a big store up in Liverpool, and they all seem to be enjoying themselves in their own way. It wouldn't be so bad if we made a raid on all the transistors and threw them into the sea. The best thing is to get out of range of the infernal things, and find some quiet spot over the cliff.'

'I've already realised that,' McLean said.

A very bronzed young woman came into the bar where they were talking. She was seven-eighths naked, and quite obviously proud of her vital statistics.

'Phew – it's hot,' she said to the bartender, as she propped herself on a high stool near the counter. 'Have you seen that husband of mine, George?'

'No, ma'am. He hasn't been in this morning.'

'Well, give me the usual – make it a double.'

The bartender poured out the double gin, and booked it to her since she had no means of carrying any money. She sank it in a couple of draughts, rearranged her diminutive brassiere, and then stood up.

'If he comes in tell him I've been looking for him, and that he can find me by the swimming-pool. Okay?'

'Yes, ma'am. I'll tell him.'

George shrugged his shoulders as she disappeared through the doorway.

'She's always looking for her husband,' he said. 'I wouldn't be missing so much if I was him.'

'Who is she?' McLean asked.

'Mrs Bracknell. Her husband is about twice her age, and lousy with money. I bet I know where I could find him, but mum's the word.'

It was about ten minutes later, when McLean was about to take his walk, that a bald-headed man of about fifty years of age entered the bar with two other men, whom McLean had not seen before. He ordered a bottle of champagne and when the bartender was serving the party, he said:

'Your wife was asking for you a short while ago, Mr Bracknell. She said you would find her by the swimming-pool.'

'Thanks, George!' Bracknell replied. 'It won't hurt her to wait a bit on a gorgeous day like this.'

McLean then left, and made his way through the noisy crowd on the beach to a footpath which went to the top of the high cliff, and finally gave a splendid view of the coast westward. Very soon the noisy crowd was out of sight and out of mind. Now the only sounds which met his ears were those of the sea and the sea birds. He walked on and on until he realised he had now gone too far to be in time for luncheon at the hotel.

A mile or so further on he came to a small inn, and decided to have a drink there and find out what they could do in the way of food. The answer was satisfactory and soon he was sitting in a small room, with two other walkers, enjoying the best meal he had had for some time.

It was early evening when he arrived back at the noisy hotel, and after an hour or so of well-earned rest he went downstairs to the evening meal. Mayhew was already sitting at the table which they shared.

'Did you dodge the madding crowd?' he asked.

'I did indeed. Did you?'

'Yes. I motored out to a golf course, about six miles from here, and found another lone man who wanted a game. He didn't tell me he had a handicap of two, but I soon found out. He murdered me,' Mayhew said. 'Ah, here comes the siren of the double-gins. All alone too.'

Mrs Bracknell gave them a nod and a smile as she made for her table, and sat down. She wore the latest thing in evening gowns which revealed almost as much as her bikini had. She waved the waiter away when he came to serve her, but finally she beckoned him.

'Looks very annoyed,' Mayhew said. 'I wouldn't mind betting he's still in the bar, sinking whatever his drink is at this time of the day.'

When they had finished their meal Bracknell was still absent, and his wife now looked furious. She spoke for some time to the waitress who was serving coffee, and when the girl came to McLean's table the irrepressible Mayhew asked her if Bracknell was unwell.

'No, sir,' she said in a low voice. 'I think they have had a row. He didn't come in to lunch, and she's in a bad temper.'

Not much of Mrs Bracknell was seen later in the evening. There was a dance on and the hotel was bedlam. McLean who couldn't stand the noise went for a stroll in the grounds, and was returning to the hotel in the gloaming when a police car arrived, and from it stepped a uniformed inspector and a sergeant. The Inspector stared at McLean in astonishment.

'Well, I'm dashed!' he said. 'Fancy meeting you here.'

'You're no more surprised than I am, Spencer,' McLean said. 'But I'm on holiday, and you apparently are on business. What's it all about?'

'A man has been found in the sea at Long Point, about two miles from here. He died from a knife wound in his back, and not from drowning. No identification so far, but on his undervest was a name-tape – Herbert Bracknell. We have been telephoning the hotels in the vicinity, and have just heard that a man of that name is staying here, but has been absent for two meals. Do you know him?'

'Yes. I suppose you want someone to identify him?'

'That's the idea.'

'Then I'd better come back with you. I should like to have a word with your chief. It may help the investigation.'

'It certainly might. Jump in.'

106

II

When McLean saw the corpse there was no doubt at all that he was Bracknell. Nothing had been found in the pockets of the clothing, but the murderer had overlooked the name-tape on the undervest. The medical opinion was that he had been dead from six to eight hours.

'What do you suggest, Inspector?' the superintendent asked him. 'Would you like to have this case?'

'Indirectly, yes, but I do not want to be brought into it openly, because I am likely to learn more as a supposedly private and disinterested person. Give the investigation to one of your force, and leave me to gain what information I can. But better speak to my chief at Scotland Yard and get his approval if you yourself approve.'

'I do indeed. I take it you are absolutely incognito at the hotel?'

'Yes.'

'Good! I'll talk to Scotland Yard now.'

After a fairly long conversation the superintendent hung up the receiver.

'You're in, McLean,' he said. 'Spencer will be very pleased to work with you. It's a long time since we had a murder on our hands, and I wish you the best of luck.'

On their way back to the hotel Spencer was told the programme, and approved it heartily.

'Who's my first witness?' he asked.

'Mrs Bracknell. She's a sexy type of woman and was apparently not on the best of terms with her husband. Get all the information you can about his affairs. I'll see what I can get from George the barman. He appears to know them very well.'

When they reached the hotel Spencer went directly to the manager to tell him that the dead man had now been positively identified, and the worried manager put a small private room at his disposal for the purpose of taking evidence, and he and his young sergeant were soon very busy.

It did not take long for many of the guests to realise that something was wrong. Mayhew who had been dancing came to McLean and drew him aside.

'I've just heard an extraordinary rumour,' he said. 'Somebody told me that the police are here enquiring about Bracknell. They're in the room at the back of the Reception, and Mrs Bracknell has been with them for some time.'

'What's he done – robbed a bank?' McLean asked.

'I wouldn't put that past him. But it's all very queer.'

It was about half an hour later when the hotel manager came to McLean and admitted that the investigation was taking place and that the investigating officer wished to question McLean. McLean expressed surprise and was then taken to the room where Spencer was seated at a table, with his assistant, who was taking notes, but was wise to the situation.

'I've seen Mrs Bracknell,' Spencer said. 'She fainted when I told her what had happened to her husband. According to her he was a bookmaker in a big way, living with her at Southampton. In addition he ran a chain of betting shops in the southern area. She says she last saw him this morning at breakfast and that she came into the American Bar at eleven o'clock in the hope of seeing him there. She left word with the bartender to tell her husband where she could be found, but he never turned up.'

'That's correct,' McLean said. 'I and Mr Mayhew were there at the time. Later Bracknell came in with two other men. I don't know their names, but George the barman will. I want to have a quiet word with him so don't call him yet.'

Outside in the hall Mayhew was talking to one of the hotel staff, in undertones. When the man left he came across to McLean.

'That fellow has let the cat out of the bag,' he said. 'The police have found Bracknell's body. He was murdered.'

'So I gathered,' McLean said. 'I've just been questioned by the police.'

'But what on earth can you know about it?'

'You and I appear to be among the last persons to have seen Bracknell alive, with the exception of those two men who came into the bar with him for drinks. Do you know them?'

'No. I don't think I've seen them before. But George will probably know them. They seemed to know him.'

A little later McLean gazed into the bar. It was empty except for two women who were talking in hushed tones to George. They left as McLean approached the counter.

'A scotch and soda,' he said.

George served the drink and was obviously in the mood for conversation.

'I supposed you've heard the bad news?' McLean asked.

'Yes, it's all over the hotel now.'

'It must have happened soon after Mr Mayhew and I left here this morning,' McLean said. 'Did you know those two men who came in with him?'

'I've seen them before, but they're not staying in the hotel. I don't know their names.'

'I expect the police will want to trace them,' McLean said. 'Because it looks as if they were the last persons known to have seen Bracknell alive. Did they stay here long drinking after I left?'

'Only about a quarter of an hour.'

'After Mrs Bracknell had called here, asking after her husband you said you had a pretty good idea where he could be found. Why didn't you tell her?'

'I didn't think it was my business. You see, I discovered by accident that Mr Bracknell and those two men were using the old summerhouse for a quiet gamble. It's behind the tennis courts, and nobody ever goes there. I went there to find a spare table for the bar, and there they were playing poker for large stakes. There were wads of fivers lying about. Mr Bracknell slipped a one-pound note into my hand, and put a finger across his lips. I knew what he meant.'

'I think you should tell the police if they should question you,' McLean said.

George nodded his head, as several other noisy guests entered the bar.

III

The dance had finished, and most of the guests had gone to bed when McLean saw Inspector Spencer again. Nothing of importance had cropped up in the evidence which he had taken. McLean then told him what he had learnt from George, and Spencer stroked his chin reflectively.

'We've got to find those two men, but how?' he asked.

'We'll use the B.B.C.,' McLean said. 'If they hear the broadcast and are innocent I feel sure they will come forward. If they don't we must draw our own conclusions. Can I see your notes, Sergeant?' McLean asked.

The sergeant handed over his notebook, in which were many pages of neat shorthand which McLean was able to read without any trouble.

'I should like to read the statements in full in order to fix them in my mind,' McLean

112

said. 'Can I borrow the book until tomorrow morning after which you can make the typed copies.'

'Of course,' Spencer said. 'I'll get that broadcast laid on, and will meet you here tomorrow morning.'

McLean sat up late in his bedroom, carefully going over the numerous statements, especially Mrs Bracknell's evidence. She said she had married Bracknell five years previously, and that her husband had treated her well. She knew of no one who bore him any ill-will, and shortly after their marriage her husband had made a will in her favour, which was lodged with his bank in Southampton.

Amongst the other statements was one from Mayhew, who had presumably been called after McLean had last seen him. It confirmed what McLean had already told Spencer, and gave the time of their parting as 11.30, after which he had motored out to the golf course, staying there until about six in the evening. He was not a member of the club, and had paid a green fee.

McLean was having his breakfast early the following morning when Spencer turned up with some important information. The late night broadcast had been successful. One of the two men had telephoned to say that he and his brother were obviously the two men referred to.

'I went to see them,' Spencer said. 'They have a complete alibi from noon onwards. They admit the gambling, and say that on that morning Bracknell won over five hundred pounds from them. It makes one doubt if anyone in the hotel is in any way involved in the murder.'

'That may be so,' McLean agreed. 'Now I want to have a look in the place where they were playing. Better come with me.'

They went out into the spacious grounds, and finally found the old summerhouse. It was half full of deck chairs and other occasional furniture, and the floor was littered with stubbed-out cigarettes and ash.

'Litter louts,' McLean said, disgustedly. 'They might at least have kept the place tidy.'

He stooped and picked up a flimsy piece of green paper, which was being blown by the wind which came through the open door. He straightened it out and found that it was a green fee ticket issued by the Maplethorpe Golf Club for the previous day.

'Interesting,' he said. 'It's probable that a

number of people in the hotel use that golf course. There's no name on the ticket but the secretary of the club may remember the man who bought it. Let's run out there now.'

The club was only three miles distant, and when they saw the secretary in his office he said he had issued the ticket to a big blond player who went out to find someone who wanted a game. He never saw him again.

'At what time was this?' McLean asked.

'Quite early – round about ten o'clock.'

'How was he dressed?'

'A rather loud sports jacket over a grey roll-collar pullover and beige slacks. I noticed he had a slight limp.'

'Thank you,' McLean said. 'You have been very helpful.'

Spencer stared at McLean when they were outside the office entering their car.

'You seemed quite satisfied,' he said.

'Up to a point. I know a guest at the hotel who was dressed exactly as described when I saw him yesterday morning. Last night you took a statement from him. His name is Stephen Mayhew.'

'That's right. But he said he had been with you in the bar just before he went out to play golf.'

'That's not borne out by the statement of the club secretary. He must have already been to the golf course before he saw me, and that makes all the difference. I think he was trying to prove an alibi, and made rather a bad job of it. Did those two men who gambled with Bracknell say how they paid their losses?'

'Yes. The older brother – Sydney Walsh – said he called at his bank on his way here, and cashed a cheque for £500. They lost it all.'

'I'd like you to check up on that. Find out the name of his bank, and if possible the numbers of the notes. I've got to keep my tabs on Mayhew. But before you leave tell the manager to hang on to his baggage and his car. It's not unlikely that he will leave very suddenly.'

'I'll do that,' Spencer said.

It was later when McLean saw Mayhew sitting in the lounge, reading a newspaper.

'Good morning,' he said. 'It's in the newspaper – about Bracknell, I mean. Marvellous how quick they are to get to know of these things.'

'Not so marvellous when so many of the guests have been questioned, and in a small place like this where news travels quickly.

Can I see that newspaper?'

'Yes, of course.'

He handed the newspaper to McLean and indicated the paragraph referred to. McLean was reading it when the receptionist entered the lounge.

'Excuse me,' she said. 'A telegram for you, Mr Mayhew. The boy is waiting to know if there is any reply.'

Mayhew slipped open the envelope and read the telegram.

'No reply,' he said.

The girl left and Mayhew slipped the telegram into his pocket.

'Bad news from home,' he said. 'My sister has been taken ill, and I am advised to go home at once. That would have to happen on my holiday. Come and have a drink before I tell the manager to prepare my bill.'

They went into the bar where George was very busy polishing glasses.

'What's it to be?' Mayhew asked.

'It's a bit early for me,' McLean said.

'Let's go the whole hog and share a small bottle of champagne. We're not likely to meet again.'

McLean nodded and George produced the drink and two glasses. Mayhew extracted a five-pound note from his wallet, and George the change. Mayhew gave him a ten-shilling note.

'I'm leaving shortly,' he explained.

'I'm sorry to hear that, Mr Mayhew,' George said. 'I thought you were staying another week.'

'So did I,' Mayhew replied. 'Well, Mr McLean, here's the best of luck to you.'

'The same to you,' McLean said.

The wine was quickly consumed, and Mayhew looked up at the clock.

'I shall have to go,' Mayhew said. 'It was pleasant knowing you. See you perhaps before I leave.'

'I hope so.'

As soon as he had left McLean went across to George, and made what to George was an astonishing request.

'I should like to have that fiver which Mr Mayhew gave you,' he said. 'I'll give you another in exchange.'

'That's okay with me,' George said.

McLean then left the bar and found a seat in the vestibule where he sat anxiously waiting for the return of Spencer. To his great relief he arrived a few minutes later and came across to McLean.

'I've got the numbers of the notes,' he said. 'They were all new ones, and in sequence.

118

Half in tenners and half in fivers.'

'It's the fivers I'm interested in. Have a look at this one paid to George over the bar. See if it fits in.'

'It does,' Spencer said, as he referred to his notebook. 'That was smart of you.'

'Not very. From the evidence it was obvious that the man who killed Bracknell must have known he was carrying a great deal of money – what he had won from those two men, and what he already had. That may have been the prime motive...'

He stopped as suddenly Mayhew appeared. He looked pale and angry and made towards the exit door.

'Get him,' McLean said. 'He may go directly to his car.'

Spencer was in time to intercept Mayhew.

'I must ask you to come to police headquarters with me, Mr Mayhew,' he said. 'I have some questions to ask you in the matter of the murder of Mr Bracknell. Will you come too, Inspector?' he asked McLean.

Mayhew stared at McLean in speechless amazement, and walked between them to the police car. After lodging him at police headquarters McLean and Spencer came back to the hotel, and entered the bedroom which Mayhew had occupied. There in the smaller of his two suitcases they found a locked box in which was nearly a thousand pounds in new banknotes, nearly half of which bore numbers which were in Spencer's list.

'That appears to cook his goose completely,' McLean said. 'We shall probably never know the full details of the killing. But apparently Bracknell went back to the summerhouse, after he had seen his fellow gamblers off, and Mayhew followed him there.'

It was after Mayhew had been charged that McLean discovered that his real name was Bastone, and that he had served two prison sentences previously. He had no sister and had sent the telegram himself.

'Good work, Spencer!' McLean said.

'Me? I was never much more than an errand boy,' Spencer said. 'Anyway we got him and that's all that matters.'

7

What Happened to Enid

I

Colonel Wentworth gazed with enmity at the colourful poster in the bar of the 'Huntsman' Inn near to his home at Sandgate in Sussex. It stated that the world-renowned Bayton Circus would be on view for a whole week as from Monday August the third, in the Long Meadow at South Farm.

'Good morning, Colonel,' the innkeeper said. 'It looks as if you are going to have some noisy neighbours for a while.'

'A damned intrusion,' the Colonel growled. 'That field comes right up to my garden wall. For three years I've suffered this infernal invasion.'

'Can't you do something about it?'

'Apparently not. I've been to the Rural District Council to protest, but they wouldn't listen. I've even tried to buy that

121

field, but with no success. For a whole week life in my house will be hell, with that ghastly roundabout churning out pop music fortissimo. Give me a double whisky.'

The innkeeper served the drink, while the Colonel let off a lot more steam. He was in the mood to tear the poster down, but had another double whisky instead, and finally made his way home through the pleasant peaceful country lanes.

On reaching his very nice house he told his daughter, Enid, who kept house for him, the doleful news, and she, being fully aware of his detestations of noisy disturbances, did her best to console him.

'It's only for a week, Daddy,' she said.

'Only a week!' he retorted. 'Two hours of it will be enough to drive me up the wall.'

'Then why not take a holiday,' she said. 'No doubt they could find you a room at the Country Club. You could play golf in the daytime and Bridge at night. Actually it would suit me too, because the house needs a spring clean, and Mrs Drummond and I could get it all spick and span by the time you came back.'

The Colonel thought over this simple solution and finally decided to adopt it. On the day before the circus and fair were due to arrive he packed a suitcase and his golf clubs into his car, and drove out to the club which was some ten miles distant. The room he had booked was on the ground floor, and he had only to open the casement window to step out to the hundred acres of well-kept links. Life now seemed a little brighter.

Two evenings later Enid rang him up to ask how he was getting on, and above the telephone conversation he could hear the horrible drone of the powerful roundabouts organ.

'I'm well out of it, my dear,' he said. 'It's quite pleasant here. I've done two rounds of golf today, and have some Bridge fixed up. How's the spring-cleaning progressing?'

'Very well indeed. I've got all the carpets up and the place looks like the Caledonian Market, but you'll like it by the time I've finished.'

It was three days later when the Colonel rang up Enid with a view to telling her that he was enjoying himself so much at the Club that he proposed to retain his room for a further week. But he was unable to get any reply, although he tried several times during the day. Finally he decided to drive over to the house and see her in person.

When he reached the house he found it

locked up and had to use his key to open the front door. The house looked very tidy, and he presumed that the spring-cleaning was now finished, but what puzzled him was the presence of the morning newspaper, lying on the mat inside the front door, and later a bottle of milk outside the kitchen door. From his bedroom window he could see the fairground thronged with a motley crowd. The organ on the roundabout was almost deafening, and he brandished his fist towards it and muttered a low curse.

It occurred to him that Enid might be in the fairground and he went downstairs and helped himself to a long whisky and soda. It was then that he discovered a cigarette-butt lying in the fireplace. That was singular since he knew that Enid never smoked. Some time later, in the dusk of evening, he found the noise unbearable, and decided to retreat to more peaceful surroundings. Before he left he scribbled a pencilled note on a sheet of writing paper, asking his daughter to telephone him as soon as she returned.

Back at the Club he got into a game of Bridge and temporarily forgot all about his abortive visit to the house. When the game finished at close on eleven o'clock he enquired if there had been any telephone call and was told there had not. Greatly concerned he went to bed, but on the following morning, after he had made another unsuccessful attempt to speak to Enid on the telephone, he drove to the house.

To his great relief the circus had gone, leaving litter all over the field. Now he noticed that there were two bottles of milk outside the kitchen door, and yet another newspaper inside the front door. Everything else was exactly as he had left it the previous evening. Ten minutes later he was at the police station, making a statement which the duty officer wrote down in a book.

'Did you think to bring a photograph of your daughter?' the sergeant asked.

'Yes. A good one, in colour, taken only a few months ago.'

He handed the snapshot to the sergeant who quizzed it, and promised immediate action. He advised the Colonel to give up his room at the Country Club, and to return to his home. This the Colonel promised to do, and half an hour later he and his baggage were back home. A few minutes later there was a ring from the kitchen door. The Colonel went and unbolted the door to find Mrs Drummond, the daily 'help' outside.

'Come in, Mrs Drummond,' he said grimly. 'I've been wanting to see you, but had no notion where you live.'

'I'm sorry I'm late,' she said. 'I tried to ring up Miss Enid yesterday morning to tell her I wasn't well and couldn't come. But there was no answer.'

'When were you last here?' the Colonel asked.

'The day before yesterday. I stayed quite late to help Miss Enid finish the spring-cleaning.'

'What do you call quite late?'

'It was half past six when I left. I think I must have overdid it a bit, for yesterday I was terribly sick.'

'I'm sorry about that,' the Colonel said. 'Now I must tell you some bad news. My daughter is missing, and the police are taking up the matter.'

Mrs Drummond opened her eyes wide with amazement.

'Missing!' she gasped.

'It is evident that she has not slept here for the past two nights, and naturally I am very distressed. Did she show any signs of worry when you last saw her?'

'Oh no, sir. She was very pleased with the work we had done.'

'Did she have any visitors during my absence?'

'Not while I was here.'

'I want to show you something. Come with me into the sitting-room.'

He led her into the room and then showed her the cigarette-stub which he had since transferred into an ash-tray.

'I found that in the fireplace,' he said. 'Do you know how it got there?'

'No. It was certainly not there when I left. I don't smoke and nor does Miss Enid.'

II

Shortly afterwards a police sergeant and a constable arrived in a car from county headquarters. The sergeant said that they had made the usual routine search for anyone resembling Enid who might have been the victim of a road accident and taken to hospital, perhaps unconscious, but without success.

The sergeant was then told about the cigarette-end the Colonel passed the object to him. The sergeant, whose eyes were much keener than the Colonel's examined it with great care.

'Smoked by a woman,' he said. 'There's just a trace of lipstick on it. Perhaps you didn't notice that?'

'I didn't,' the Colonel admitted. 'But no one in this house smokes cigarettes.'

'Then it would appear that your daughter entertained some woman, after the time when the daily "help" left her the day before yesterday, and that woman must have been one of the last persons to have seen her.'

'I suppose so,' the Colonel said. 'But I haven't the slightest idea who the woman might be.'

'Have I your permission to search your daughter's bedroom in the hope of finding some clue there?'

The Colonel hesitated. He disliked the idea very much but realised the request was not unreasonable in the circumstances.

'Go ahead,' he said. 'But I'll come with you.'

The subsequent search brought to light a number of letters from friends of his daughter but nothing more substantial.

'I won't trouble you any more at the moment,' the sergeant said. 'I'll get in touch with the writers of the letters and will see you again later.'

Two days passed before the Colonel heard from the police that none of the letter writers had seen his daughter for some weeks. Now almost sick with anxiety he went in person to see the Chief Constable, whom he knew well, and demanded further action in the matter, whereupon that gentleman promised to enlist the aid of Scotland Yard.

It was on the following morning that Inspector McLean and his assistant, Sergeant Brook, called at the house. The Colonel liked the look of McLean. There was something dynamic about him which had the effect of causing the Colonel's drooping spirit to rise a little.

'I presume you have not received any communication from your daughter – or concerning her?' McLean asked.

'Not a word. At first I thought she might have been kidnapped perhaps for ransom, but if that had happened surely I should have heard from the persons responsible?'

'I think you would,' McLean agreed. 'But are you quite sure that nothing of value has been removed from the house?'

'Quite sure.'

'Tell me about your daughter. Has she

always lived here with you?'

'Only since my wife died four years ago. Up to then she was a Ward Sister in St Mary's Hospital in Kensington. She resigned in order to look after me. I am quite capable of looking after myself, but she insisted and I gave way.'

'Has she ever been married, or engaged to be married?'

'No.'

'I know that the county police have examined her bedroom here, but discovered nothing of importance. I should like to see that room myself.'

The Colonel nodded and directed McLean and Brook to the room in question, and then left them there alone. The subsequent search was much more thorough than that made by the Colonel and the local officer, for in a trinket box McLean found an engagement ring of good quality.

'Could have belonged to her mother,' McLean ruminated. 'But the Colonel will probably know.'

The Colonel, when questioned about this, was taken aback. He said his late wife had a very different engagement ring which was sold with some other jewellery after her death. He had never seen the present ring before.

McLean's next quest was at the hospital where Enid had been employed. The matron there was most complimentary about the late Ward Sister.

'She was excellent in every respect,' she said, 'and we were sorry when she left in order to look after her father. But I know practically nothing of her private life.'

'Is there anyone here who will remember her?' McLean asked.

'Yes, indeed. There is the Almoner – Miss Ansell – she and Enid were very close friends. They shared a small flat quite close to the hospital. She's available if you would like to see her.'

McLean said he would, and he and Brook were taken to the Almoner's office, and introduced to her.

'I think you may be able to help me, Miss Ansell,' McLean said. 'I am investigating the disappearance of Miss Enid Wentworth, who once worked here. I am informed you knew her well.'

'Yes – quite well,' she replied.

'Was she at any time engaged to a man?'

'I'm not sure about that,' she said. 'There was a man she was very friendly with. She

131

brought him home to our flat once or twice, and then suddenly it all ended. When I mentioned him to her some time afterwards she made it fairly obvious that she did not want to discuss him, and she seemed to be very cut-up.'

'Do you remember his name?'

'Yes. It was Horace Winterton.'

'Do you know where he can be found?'

'No. Oh, wait a moment. I believe she wrote his telephone number on the telephone chart in the flat.'

'Do you still occupy the same flat?'

'Yes.'

'I should very much like to know that number. Could you possibly come with me now to the flat?'

Miss Ansell said she would provided she had the Matron's consent. The Matron, when questioned, had no objection and very soon they were in the flat and in possession of the telephone number.

III

Back at Scotland Yard McLean put a call through to the number in question, which was on the Emberbrook exchange, and not yet on the automatic system. A woman's voice was heard on the other end of the line.

'Can I speak to Mr Winterton?' McLean asked.

'I think you must have the wrong number,' the woman said. 'There is no Mr Winterton here.'

'It's the number I have. This is a police enquiry. May I ask your name and address?'

'Yes. It is Mrs Drake of number six Westmoreland Terrace, Ditton. I bought the house three years ago.'

'I should like to see you in the matter. Would that be convenient in about an hour's time?'

'Yes, but I don't think I can help you.'

McLean said he would take a chance, and an hour later he was ringing the bell at a terrace house. A middle-aged woman came to the door.

'I am the police officer who telephoned a short time ago,' he said. 'I'm sorry to trouble you.'

'That's quite all right. Please come in.'

McLean and Brook entered a neat little sitting-room where McLean explained his mission.

'We are very anxious to trace a Mr Horace Winterton, who presumably lived here

133

before you came,' he said. 'Will you tell me from whom you bought the house?'

'Yes. It was advertised by a house agent in Kingston – a Mr Young. I called on him – in Clarence Street, and he showed me over the house. I liked it and eventually bought it.'

'Did he never mention the previous owner?'

'Not by name, but whoever he was he left the house in a very dirty state.'

It was soon clear that Mrs Drake knew absolutely nothing about Winterton, and McLean thanked her, and went in search of the house agent, whom he found in his office.

'Yes, I sold that house to Mrs Drake,' he said. 'Mr Winterton was there before her.'

'What sort of a man was he?' McLean asked.

'Most queer. I saw him a number of times, and could never get to the bottom of him. He looked quite sane, but at times he'd go clean off his rocker. A good-looking fellow. Quite a pin-up character.'

'Have you ever seen him with this young woman?' McLean asked, and showed him a photograph which he had got from the county police.

'Yes, I think I have, but I can't remember

when or in what circumstances.'

'Do you know where he is living now?'

'No. But while the house was up for sale I had some letters from him from a hotel where he was staying. It was called Holly-croft, Berryland Road, Surbiton. They may know where he went from there.'

McLean thanked him and was soon at the small private hotel. The proprietress had good reason to remember Winterton.

'He had a chip on his shoulder,' she said. 'I was glad when he left here, because some of my permanent guests threatened to leave if he stayed on any longer.'

'What was wrong with him?' McLean asked.

'I thought it was drink, but then I discovered that it was dope. I was about to tell him that he couldn't have his room any longer when he suddenly left on his own account.'

'When was this?' McLean asked.

'About three years ago.'

'Do you know where he went?'

'No. But recently my cook told me she saw him in the garden of an old house near Ewell, where her mother lives. He didn't appear to see her, but she swore it was him.'

When McLean saw the cook she stuck to

her story, and told him exactly where the house was.

'It's like a game of hunt-the-slipper,' Brook commented when they were on the road again.

They had little difficulty in finding the house. It was very old and decrepit, and was called 'Woodlands'. Brook drove the car close up to the front door, and he and McLean got out and rang the door-bell. After trying several times without response they went round the corner of the house, and found a garage door – wide open. The back door of the house, like the front, was locked, but farther down the garden a bonfire was burning. They walked to it, and discovered that it had not long been lighted.

'He can't be far away,' McLean said. 'We had better wait a bit.'

They were walking back to their car when McLean heard a banging which appeared to come from inside the house. He looked up and noticed that one of the top attic windows was boarded up.

'It seems to come from up there,' he said.

The banging ceased for a few moments and then started again. Now McLean was certain that the sound came from behind the boarded window. They walked round the

136

house seeking for some easy means of entry, but found none. Then suddenly a car appeared in the drive. It came at tremendous speed and narrowly missed hitting the police car.

'Darned idiot!' Brook ejaculated.

The driver of the car got out, and stared at the two intruders. His face was deathly pale, and his dark eyes glinted strangely.

'You shouldn't leave your car there,' he snapped. 'Who are you anyway?'

'Police officers,' McLean said. 'You, I presume, are Mr Winterton. I have some questions to ask you. Open the door.'

'You can't give me orders. Ask your questions here.'

'Open that door or I shall take you to police headquarters and get the key from you there.'

Winterton stood his ground with his fists clenched. Brook looked at McLean meaningly, and McLean nodded. The next moment Brook's powerful arms held Winterton pinioned, and McLean removed the door-key from his jacket pocket.

'Bring him in, Brook,' he said, as he unlocked the door. 'Look after him while I investigate that room upstairs.'

While Brook half-carried the struggling

man to a room just inside the front door McLean went up to the attic. The door was locked on the outside, but the key was still in the lock. McLean knocked and then entered. There he found the missing girl standing by the boarded window, with one shoe in her hand, the heel of which she had used to give the alarm.

'It's all right, Miss Wentworth,' McLean said. 'I am a police officer. Are you all right?'

'Yes. I've been well fed and looked after. I was kidnapped while my father was away.'

'Was it Winterton who did that?'

'Yes, it's rather a sad story. I was in love with him for a while – engaged in fact. But then I discovered that he was mentally deranged, and a secret drug addict. At our last meeting, before I left the hospital, I had to tell him that the engagement was off. Later I returned the engagement ring by registered post, but to my surprise it came back to me by the dead-letter post. I never saw him again until that evening when after an old girl friend had left he called at our house in a car. He told me he had been in a mental clinic, but was now quite cured. But he didn't look cured to me. I told him it was quite useless and that I intended to stay with my father as long as he lived. It was then that he went quite mad, and carried me, struggling, out to his car. You know the rest.'

'Did he tell you what he intended to do with you?'

'He – he said he would never let me go. I belonged to him and always would. He said he would kill anyone who tried to take me from him. You can't think how terrible it was.'

'I think I can,' McLean said. 'He's downstairs now, but if you would prefer not to see him I'll take him away and then come and drive you home.'

'Do that,' she begged. 'I can't stand any more. When you've gone I'll ring up and tell my father the good news.'

It was an hour later when McLean returned and had the joy of taking her back to her father, who had already been told over the telephone what had happened.

'What's to become of that man?' he asked McLean.

'It's certain he will be found unfit to plead. I don't think you need worry any more about him, Miss Wentworth. Perhaps after expert treatment he will really be cured.'

When McLean said goodbye Miss Wentworth's hand gripped his for quite a few moments more than were really necessary, and her lovely brown eyes were eloquent of her heart-felt gratitude.

8

The Baby-sitter

I

The Sufflings were far from being a happy family and the reason was not far to seek. The old man – Edward – had done his best to prevent his son – George – from marrying Sandra Watcombe but to no purpose. Young George was headstrong and plunged into marriage despite the objections.

'Father thinks we can't make a do of it on my small salary,' he said to Sandra. 'But I told him you were prepared to keep your present job until I was earning more money. I know that housing is the difficulty, but we'll find something.'

But they found nothing in the shape of unfurnished houses, and finally took a very small furnished flat at a most inflated rent.

For two years they managed to pay their way, and then Sandra found there was a baby coming, and in a few months she had to give up her job. The rent of the flat was now beyond their means and finally George had to go to his father and admit it. The old man's solution was that they should come and live with him until such time as they could get an unfurnished house of their own.

Now they had been at the big house for two years, and Sandra with a baby on her hands was quite unable to add to the family income. She grew more and more unhappy for she and the housekeeper hit it off badly.

'We must get out of here, George,' she said. 'Mrs Chapman is dreadful. Nothing I do is right, and your father sides with her. Try to find some place, darling, if it's only two rooms.'

George did try but with no success, until he heard that a charming little cottage in the village was for sale. He took Sandra to see it and she was enraptured. Everything was just right. There was a nice little garden, and the bus into town stopped almost at the door.

'It would be Paradise,' she said. 'But what's the use? We have only two hundred pounds in the bank and you told me the lowest price for the cottage is £2,000.'

'I know. I went to the bank and had a chat with the manager. I've known him all my life. He told me he was sure he could put me on to a Building Society who would advance £1,500. We should need our savings to buy furniture. If we could raise the other £500 we could get the place.'

'If pigs had wings they might fly.'

George shut his mouth grimly. He, like Sandra, was sick of the present set-up. He knew little about his father's means, but he was certain that he wasn't hard up for five hundred pounds.

'I'm going to have a heart-to-heart talk with Father,' he said.

He carried out his intention that evening, after they had had the evening meal and Sandra was busy upstairs. His father listened a little impatiently and then shook his head.

'I can't do it, George,' he said. 'Even if I had the money to lend you, I don't think it would be wise for you to take on such commitments on your present small income. You young people must learn to live within your means. I had to when I was your age.'

George argued valiantly – almost angrily, but it was useless, and finally he went back to his wife, who knew by the expression on his face that he had failed.

'Nothing doing?' she asked.

'No. I don't understand him. It isn't as if I expected him to give me the money. I told him I would repay him monthly but nothing would melt him.'

'Perhaps he hasn't got five hundred pounds,' said Sandra.

'I know he has. He's just a skinflint. It was the same when Mother was alive. There was always trouble about the housekeeping bills. The fact is he likes taking it out of me because I – I...'

He stopped as Sandra looked at him strangely.

'Because you married me,' said Sandra quietly. 'I've tried to make him like me. I thought that when I presented him with a grandson he might soften his heart, but he seems to have no interest at all in my darling baby.'

The months passed and things grew worse rather than better. In order to raise money and save enough for them to be able to pay the deposit on a home of their own Sandra got an evening job in a restaurant which meant that George saw practically nothing of her except at week-ends. George, watching his wife working herself to death, grew desperate.

It was in the autumn that Inspector McLean was instructed to go to the small village of Speke in Surrey to investigate the murder of Edward Suffling whose body had been found in a ditch only a few hundred yards from his house. The County Constabulary had already taken some evidence, but now requested Scotland Yard to take over the case. McLean read the depositions before leaving in a car for Speke.

'An old man struck down in a country lane,' he said to Sergeant Brook. 'Motive apparently not robbery for the victim's wallet had ten pounds in it. Son and daughter-in-law living in the same house. Will found in favour of son, and evidence to suggest that there was considerable friction between this couple and the murdered man. Medical evidence is that Suffling died between eight and nine o'clock on Tuesday evening. Well, let's go. We'll call at county headquarters on the way and find out if there has been any additional information.'

The County Inspector who had carried out the preliminary investigation was unable to add much to what had already been stated. There was, however, one fact which had emerged which he thought worth mentioning.

'Some months ago young George Suffling was interested in a cottage in the village which was for sale,' he said. 'He went to the bank to see if he could raise a loan or a mortgage. The manager was able to help him to some extent, but he still required another five hundred pounds. The manager, who knew that old Suffling had considerable securities at the bank, suggested that George talk it over with his father. He never heard from George again, so presumably the old man wouldn't play.'

'Do you know the son personally?' McLean asked.

'No. I had never met him until yesterday when I questioned him. But I knew the old man.'

'Did he ever speak about his son?'

'Very seldom. I got the impression that they weren't on very good terms. The son is employed in an estate agent's office in this town – Willoughbys. They're not doing very well and the boy's position is not very secure.'

II

McLean and Brook proceeded to Speke, taking with them a young detective from the County C.I.D. Just before they reached the Suffling house the car stopped and the detective indicated the spot where the body had been found. It was in a hollow lane fringed by high hedgerows. The deep ditch on one side showed the impression made by the body, and where the head had rested there was blood mixed with the heavy mud. On the road there was also some dried blood.

'Must have been around dusk when it happened,' said the detective. 'The body was found by Jim Waters, a farm labourer who has a cottage further down the lane. That was at ten-thirty, and it was by luck that the ray from his torch fell on it. We searched for footprints but had no luck.'

After a few minutes McLean went on to the house where the young detective introduced him to Mrs Chapman, the somewhat dour housekeeper. He was informed that both George and his wife were in the house.

He had a copy of the statement made by Mrs Chapman, but decided he would check up on it.

'When Mr Suffling left the house at seven-twenty did he not give you any idea when he would return?' McLean asked.

'No. But he always had a meal at eight o'clock and I expected him back then.'

'Did he often take a walk at that time?'

'No, but he had a telephone call earlier and I thought it might have had something to do with that.'

'Did you hear anything that was said?'

'No.'

'After Mr Suffling had gone out who was left in the house?' McLean asked.

'Only myself and Mr George. Mrs Suffling was at work at the Corona Café in the town. She goes there after the baby is asleep and usually gets home round about ten o'clock.'

'You have said that soon after old Mr Suffling had left his son asked you if you would keep your ears open for the baby in case he cried, as he had to keep an appointment.'

'That's right. He said he thought he would be back in an hour. I heard him start up his motor-bike soon afterwards.'

'But he didn't return for two hours?'

'Just about that. He asked me if the baby had woke up and I told him I hadn't heard a sound.'

147

'Did he appear to be quite normal?'

Mrs Chapman hesitated as if the question troubled her.

'I – I thought he looked a little troubled,' she said. 'But I put it down to his worrying about the baby, because he usually stayed here while his wife was at work.'

'Was he surprised when his father did not return?'

'Very surprised. He said he couldn't think what had happened to him to miss his supper and be out so late.'

'Is it true that of late there has been a great deal of family friction?'

'Unfortunately, yes. Mr George and his wife have never settled down here. They've always wanted a place of their own, but could never afford it.'

'Did you know that Mr George had tried to borrow money from his father?'

'No, but I guessed there had been a quarrel because for weeks they have scarcely spoken to each other.'

A little later McLean saw George in another room. He was pallid and his mouth twitched as Sergeant Brook produced a note-book and pencil.

'Mr Suffling,' said McLean. 'It is in evidence that you left this house on Tuesday evening soon after your father had gone out and that you were absent for two hours. You have stated that you had to keep an appointment. With whom did you make that appointment?'

'That – that was not strictly true,' replied George in a low husky voice. 'The fact is I was sick of staying in night after night babywatching, while my wife was working. I just wanted an hour or so of freedom, so I took my motorbike and went off.'

'Did you meet anybody during that time?'

'No.'

'Didn't you call at any pub?'

'No. I just kept on riding and got as far as the south downs from where I could see the sea. I got back here at ten o'clock and Mrs Chapman told me that my father had not returned.'

'In the evidence already given you did not reveal that you and your father had quarrelled recently.'

'We did not quarrel.'

'But you were not on very good terms?'

'No.'

'Was it because you asked him to lend you money, and he refused?'

'Yes. My wife has never been happy here, chiefly because she and the housekeeper cannot get on together. I thought my father would help me in the purchase of a cottage, and he refused.'

'Can you think of any reason why anyone should murderously assault your father?'

'No, I can't. But if you think I am capable of murdering my father you are making a big mistake.'

'Please confine yourself to answering my questions,' said McLean. 'Did you know that your father had made you the chief beneficiary under a will.'

'No. He never told me.'

McLean then saw the young wife. She was tremendously moved by the tragedy and obviously knew that her husband was suspect. She admitted the friction which had existed between son and father, and also between herself and Mrs Chapman.

'Weren't you surprised by your husband's two-hour absence from home that evening?' McLean asked.

'Yes, until he told me that he was fed up with the boredom of staying in the house every evening. I could understand that. We have both been most unhappy here.'

McLean did not press her unduly since she herself had a perfect alibi, and a little later he went to the shed where George kept his motor-bike. It was very dirty and presumably had not been used since the night of the murder. He looked at the various tools but all of them were very clean, and none of them was big enough to have inflicted the injury from which Suffling had died.

But while examining various parts of the machine McLean suddenly found something of great significance. On the underside of the right handlebar grip was a smear of blood. Brook gave a low whistle when he too saw this.

'That may take a bit of explaining,' he said.

III

George explained it later in a manner that was somewhat unconvincing.

'I – I cut my hand a little,' he said. 'I didn't know it had bled. Look, you can see the mark.'

He held up the palm of his right hand and revealed quite a minor scratch.

'How did you do that?' McLean asked.

'I – I can't think. I didn't notice it at the time.'

151

McLean had the machine removed to the police laboratory in the hope that the blood-group could be proved, but after a little while the expert said there was insufficient blood for the test to be conclusive.

George, now fully aware of what was going on, displayed ever-increasing terror which did not pass unnoticed by McLean. It was the terror of a guilty man, and yet at the same time he found it difficult to believe that the young man could kill his father in cold blood.

With Brook he went to the scene of the crime to make a thorough search of the ditch and the grass verge between it and the road. The net result of this was two sweet wrappers, bearing the word 'Balsers', trampled into the grass a few yards from where the body had lain.

'May have no connection,' said Brook. 'Anyone could have dropped them.'

'Yes, but when I was in the house questioning Mrs Chapman I saw some sweets bearing similar wrappers. They were in a bowl on the dresser. We'll go into that immediately.'

Mrs Chapman was out when they reached the house, so McLean went into the kitchen. Only two of the half-dozen sweets were left. He showed these to George.

'I've never seen them before,' said George. 'But I know that Mrs Chapman is fond of sweets.'

McLean reflected for a moment and then stared into George's tense face.

'Do you still stand by your recent statement that you took out your motor-cycle and stayed away for over two hours, with no end in view?' he asked.

George gulped and looked at his wife who was close by. She nodded her head. George switched his gaze to McLean.

'I lied,' he said. 'I did have an object in view. My wife did not know until just now when I told her. I was desperately in need of money, and I planned to rob a jeweller's shop at Haywards Heath. I had been there before and knew the set-up. The owner lived over the premises, and the lighted window had no grille. It was down a side street and no one was about. I left the bike outside, and broke the window with a hammer. I was about to remove a tray of rings from the window when suddenly a policeman appeared in the distance. I got on my machine and rode off. I don't think he was near enough to read my registration number. I think my hand was cut by a piece of flying glass. It was then a quarter past nine, and I rode home as fast as I could. That's the whole truth. I never saw my father after I left home.'

McLean had no reason to doubt that story, but he was quickly on the telephone to Haywards Heath, and was told that the constable on the beat had reported the incident at the time given by George.

When the housekeeper returned McLean took up the question of the wrapped sweets with her. She admitted that she had bought a packet of them at a cinema a few nights previously, had eaten some of them and brought the rest home.

'Did you give any of them to any other person?' McLean asked.

'Yes,' she replied. 'My son called to see me and I gave him some before he left.'

'When was that?' McLean asked.

She reflected and then began to look worried.

'Was it on the evening when Mr Suffling was killed?' McLean asked.

'Y-yes. Just after Mr George had left,' she quavered.

'Does your son often come here?'

'Not often. I hadn't seen him for six months when he called.'

'Where does he live?'

Mrs Chapman gave an address in Lambeth, and in reply to another question said that her son – Herbert – was employed in a garage near his address.

McLean felt he was now on the right scent but before going to Lambeth he saw the solicitor in the nearby town who was in possession of Suffling's will.

'To what extent does Mrs Chapman benefit?' he asked.

'If she is still in the employ of Mr Suffling she is to receive the sum of £3,000 for her long and devoted service,' replied the solicitor.

'Do you think Mrs Chapman knew that?' McLean asked.

'Yes, she knew that. Suffling told her because he didn't want to lose her.'

'Do you know anything about her son Herbert?'

'Quite enough. Suffling told me. He lost his father early in life and became unmanageable. He spent some years in a Borstal institution and came out no better than when he went in. I know he has been to prison twice since then.'

The subsequent visit to Herbert Chapman's two-room flatlet in a cheap apartment house was not immediately productive for the place was locked up. McLean then went to the garage mentioned by Mrs Chapman.

'He's not here any longer,' said the manager. 'I fired him last Saturday. I was crazy to take him on without a reference, but he told me a hard-luck story and I needed help at the pumps.'

'Why did you sack him?'

'He was robbing me but it was difficult to prove. If you want him I expect you'll find him at the "Cricketers" about this time. He drinks like a fish. It's just round the corner.'

McLean found his man in the rather lowdown pub. He was about twenty-five years of age, lean of face and dissipated. As there were other persons in the bar McLean took him in the car to Scotland Yard and questioned him there. He denied having seen Suffling on the evening when he visited his mother, and he denied knowing that she would benefit considerably by the death of her employer. When he reached the house Suffling had already gone out. His mother had told him so.

'That's true,' said McLean. 'But I suggest you waited for his return and waylaid him...'

'You're a liar!' shouted Chapman.

Sergeant Brook quickly put an end to that sort of argument, and while Chapman was still breathless he was searched. It yielded only one thing of interest. It was a pawn ticket dated the previous day for a gold watch, and the sum lent on it was £12.

Chapman was held in custody and the pawnbroker was visited. He made a wry face when McLean suggested that the watch might have been stolen, and took charge of the article after giving a receipt.

'A nice Swiss job,' said McLean. 'Must have cost sixty pounds at least. Do you think that Chapman came by this honestly?'

'But it isn't in evidence that Suffling lost a watch,' said Brook.

'Who would know? It's a pocket watch and may have fallen out of his pocket when he was trundled into that ditch. But we'll soon find out.'

George Suffling, when shown the watch, identified it at once as his father's, and Mrs Chapman confirmed this, without realising its full significance. Before McLean left George came to him.

'Am – am I in the clear now, Inspector?' he asked.

'Not quite. There's a small charge

standing against you of breaking a window with intent to commit a felony. But don't let it cause you too many sleepless nights.'

9

The Bridge Party

I

Andrew Cummings hated his young wife's parties which she gave at frequent intervals. It wasn't the expense that troubled him, but the inconvenience to which he was put. Even his little study was snatched from him to be turned into a repository for women's hats and coats, and he was expected, after a gruelling day at the office, to play Bridge until the early hours of the morning. But to please Penelope he made the best of a bad situation.

'Who is it tonight?' he asked. 'The usual crowd, I suppose?'

'Yes, you know them all, except a girl I met at the Bridge Club. She's quite charming and a very good Bridge player. You'll like her. Whatever you do don't be late home, dear. We have cocktails at seven o'clock and dinner punctually at half past.'

'I won't,' he promised.

It was some hours later at his office in London that Cummings was rung up by his wife.

'Andrew dear,' she said. 'I'm in a mess. I invited just enough people to make up four tables of Bridge, and now Mrs Baxter has rung up to tell me she has a very bad cold and can't make it. I've tried to get someone else but failed. Can you bring home someone from the office to take her place? We can easily put him up for the night.'

'I suppose he must be a Bridge player?'

'Yes, of course. That's the whole idea.'

'All right. I'll do my best.'

Later Cummings rang up Penelope to tell her it was all right and that he would bring a man with him. He and the friend arrived at the Weybridge house at half past six to find Penelope and the maid busy laying the dining-table which had been fully extended for the occasion.

'Penelope, meet John Maxwell,' said Cummings. 'He's our Canadian representative.'

Penelope shook hands with the tall good-looking man and thanked him for filling the gap, after which he and Cummings vanished to have a quiet drink on their own.

'Lovely place you've got here,' said Maxwell as he stared through the window at the flowers and the well-cut velvety lawns outside. 'A swimming-pool too. I didn't know you lived in such style.'

'It's my wife. She was blessed with a very rich father. My poor salary wouldn't run to this.'

Soon the guests began to arrive and the preliminaries got under way. Cummings knew them all with the exception of the girl whom his wife had mentioned. She was a dark beauty named Sophia Grant, daughter of an English father and an Italian mother, both of whom she had lost years before. She spoke English with just a trace of Italian accent.

'She's quite a peach,' Cummings said to his wife. 'What does she do for a living?'

'I don't think she does anything, but she's trying to start an Italian class. There's a chance for you, Andrew.'

'Thanks, but I've never really learned to talk English.'

The big room was now a babble of conversation, and Sophia came in for a lot of attention on the part of the males. Major

Wilkins who always had an eye for a pretty woman with outstanding vital statistics was doing his best to monopolise her, much to his wife's annoyance.

When dinner was announced they all moved into the dining-room where Penelope had marked their places with small cards. They occupied completely the very large table which was nicely decorated with flowers from the garden. Cummings found himself sitting next to Sophia. During the cocktails she had appeared to be very animated but now she was curiously dumb, and he had difficulty in engaging her in conversation. In the end he gave it up.

After the meal Penelope announced that the bar was open and that Bridge would start in half an hour, in the large sun-lounge. She and Cummings then went to check up on the card tables, and in due course all was ready for the great battle. It was then discovered that Sophia's table was not complete, for Sophia herself was not there.

'She's probably powdering her nose,' said Penelope. 'I'll go and find her.'

But this mission was in vain, for Sophia did not appear to be in the house.

'I saw her a little while ago in the garden,' said Major Wilkins.

'What a nuisance!' said Penelope. 'Andrew dear, find her and tell her we are all ready.'

Andrew opened the casement window and went into the garden where it was now almost dark. The place was full of shrubberies and pergolas and shady retreats where one might linger, but he saw no sign of Sophia. Below the swimming-pool there was a rustic summerhouse. It had no door, and as he was about to pass he glanced inside. Sophia was lying on the floor, half on her face. He hurried to her side, and raised her body in his arms.

'Sophia, what has...'

His voice was stilled as suddenly he saw that her neck was discoloured and swollen, and in a moment he realised that she had been strangled and was dead. Gasping with horror he ran back to the house and entered the Bridge room.

'I'm – sorry,' he stammered. 'We can't go on. Something has happened to Miss Grant. I have to telephone the police at once.'

The subsequent arrival of the police and the doctor started some embarrassing questions of the guests. Since the ladies could be ruled out by the nature of the crime, the questioning was largely confined to the men. Penelope was able to state that her husband had been with her during the whole of the interval between dinner and the assembling of the party in the sun-lounge, and the Major had a similar alibi in his wife. The movements of the other men were not so certain. All of them at some time or other, during the interval, had been in the lounge drinking, but it was difficult to prove which of them had been there all the time. No one had seen Sophia in the lounge at all after the meal.

'I think she went straight into the garden after we left the dining-room,' said Maxwell. 'I saw her in the hall for a moment, but did not see her in the lounge at all.'

'Were you there the whole time?' asked the Inspector.

'Yes, except for a few minutes when I went to the toilet.'

It was nearly midnight before the Inspector had finished taking the various statements, and the horrified guests permitted to leave. Penelope then turned to her husband with tearful eyes.

'I meant it to be a such a success,' she said. 'And to think it has ended this way. Poor Sophia! Who could have done such a terrible thing to her?'

II

Early the following morning Scotland Yard took a hand in the mysterious affair, and Inspector McLean and Sergeant Brook were sent down to county police headquarters to be brought up to date with the latest facts.

'The woman was undoubtedly strangled between half past eight and nine o'clock,' said the Superintendent. 'It could have been done by somebody in the house, but I very much doubt it, because the only people who knew the woman were fellow members of a local ladies Bridge club. It's very difficult to impute a motive for the crime on the part of any of the guests. That the culprit was a man is fairly certain for very great force was used. The murder could have been done by some intruder into the garden, who when he was discovered – perhaps in the act of stealing – got into a panic.'

'What could he have stolen – in a summerhouse?' McLean asked.

'Heaven knows, but nothing else makes any sense. Mr Cummings' guests are all well known in the district, and all extremely respectable.'

'What about the victim herself? Was she a local woman?'

'Yes. She came here two years ago, and took a furnished flat just out of town. In her handbag we found a key to the place and entered it last night. She appears to be of independent means, and to have lived for some time in Buffalo, U.S.A. But there has been no time to get more details. The flat is in a comparatively new building called Huntley House – number 16.'

'I should like to have the key,' said McLean. 'Also the transcript of the evidence already taken.'

These were handed to him, and during the ensuing drive to the Cummings' house he read the various statements. Taken altogether they were rather confusing.

'Not very well done,' he said to Brook. 'In that fatal half-hour between dinner and Bridge it's impossible to say with any certainty what persons left the lounge. Several of the men admit leaving the room for a few minutes, but the actual times are not given. The only thing that is certain is that the victim was not seen at all in the lounge after dinner, but Major Wilkins swears he saw her in the garden about five minutes after he himself entered the lounge.'

'What about the Superintendent's theory?' asked Brook.

'Something like that could happen, but not the way it did,' McLean replied. 'You can't strangle to death a healthy young woman in a few moments of panic or passion. Any able man cornered by surprise could have knocked her out with a heavy blow and got clean away. No, Brook, I think this murder was deliberate, and not without a hidden motive. Ah, this must be the house.'

Cummings, in view of the circumstances, had not gone to his office, nor had his associate Maxwell. McLean saw them both together and checked up their statements. Cummings could only repeat that he had been with his wife during the whole time between dinner and Bridge. Maxwell said that apart from his first introduction to Sophia he had not had a chance of talking to her. When he went into the lounge after dinner she wasn't there. He had not seen her in the garden as Major Wilkins appeared to have done.

Mrs Cummings like her husband had no useful evidence. She was tremendously upset by the whole terrible affair. Eventually McLean and Brook went to the scene of the crime. The summerhouse was only a short distance from the main gate, and this bore out McLean's argument that the intruder – had there been one – could have got away quite easily without committing his dreadful crime.

Outside was an area of flagstones all of which were quite dry and unmarked. Inside there were a few easy chairs clustered round a cane table. A vase which had presumably been on the table was lying on the floor in pieces with the flowers it had contained.

'There seems to have been some resistance,' mused McLean.

They spent some time in the small place but found nothing which shed any new light on the murder. They commenced to go back to the house by a different route when suddenly McLean stopped and picked up two strip matches lying within a yard of each other. One was practically unburnt, which suggested it had been blown out by the wind making it necessary for the user to strike a second. On the flat side of both matches was printed 'S.S. *Medina*'.

'Can't have been here long,' McLean mused. 'Because it rained all yesterday morning, and the matches are bone dry. Near the summerhouse too.'

The matches were placed in a box as possible exhibits, and on reaching the house McLean asked to see the maid who had helped Mrs Cummings the previous evening.

'Did you clear away the dishes in the dining-room after dinner?' he asked.

'Yes, sir.'

'You have a good view of the garden from that room, haven't you?'

'Yes, sir.'

'Did you happen to see anyone in the garden while you were there?'

'No, sir.'

This was not inconsistent with Major Wilkins' statement, since the lounge and the dining-room faced in different directions. McLean dismissed her, and then went with Brook to visit the dead woman's flat. It was a small but well-appointed place, and the subsequent search revealed one or two interesting facts. One was that the dead woman had been a heavy drinker, for a cupboard was full of empty whisky and gin bottles. Another was that she gambled heavily on horses and dogs. From various documents it appeared that she had come into some money about four years previously, and had invested it in gilt-edged securities from which she received about eight hundred pounds a year in interest. But there was a not a thing that shed any light on her past life. In a box containing small jewellery was a man's gold Hunter watch with the initials. A.M.M. on the outer case. Finally McLean was disappointed by the meagre results of the search.

'We must try elsewhere,' he said. 'I'm quite interested in those two strip matches marked "S.S. *Medina*". If one of the witnesses should have made a voyage in a ship of that name it would be significant. Get me through to Lloyd's. I've a friend there who may help.'

This friend did help considerably. He knew the vessel and the shipping company who owned it, and was able to state that the last voyage of the *Medina* was from Montreal to Liverpool where she arrived three weeks previously and was now undergoing some minor repairs. Immediately McLean got in touch with the Steamship Company, and in quick time was furnished with a full list of the passengers carried on the last voyage.

'You take the list of guests, Brook,' he said. 'And I'll read the passenger list. It will take some time.'

The names were read off rapidly, and

McLean was about half-way through when he saw a name which caused him to catch his breath.

'Wait for it, Brook,' he said. 'Here he is – Mr John Maxwell of Toronto.'

'Glory!' ejaculated Brook. 'He's the man Cummings brought down from London to make up the Bridge number.'

'Yes, the man who swore he had never even spoken to Miss Grant except for the introduction. That's very – very interesting.'

III

Cummings was in his office when McLean and Brook called an hour later. He was Publicity Manager of the concern which marketed a number of motor car accessories and he looked almost as worried as when McLean had last seen him.

'It concerns Mr Maxwell,' said McLean. 'He represents the firm in Canada, doesn't he?'

'Yes. He has an office in Toronto, but comes over for a few weeks each year for consultations.'

'How long has he been with the firm?'

'Three years.'

'Is he a Canadian?'

'No, but has lived in Canada nearly all his life.'

'Married?'

'No.'

'When you introduced him to Miss Grant did he exhibit any sign of surprise, or did she on seeing him?'

'I thought he was very impressed by her good looks and figure. But then most men would be.'

'And Miss Grant?'

'She seemed more than a bit interested in him too.'

'Is he in the office now?'

'No. He's due to leave for Liverpool tomorrow to catch a ship back to Canada. I shan't see him until tomorrow morning when he will call to pick up a parcel of advertising literature.'

'Where is he staying?'

'The Windsor Hotel in Bloomsbury.'

When they left Brook imagined that McLean would go straight to Maxwell's hotel, but McLean had other ideas.

'Back to the Yard,' he said. 'I've got some telephoning to do.'

The subsequent telephone call to Toronto took quite a time, and thereafter McLean remained in his office waiting for the upshot. It was ten o'clock that evening when at last the call came from the Toronto police. McLean, with notebook and pencil by his side wrote down in shorthand what came through. Finally he thanked the officer on the other end of the line, and hung up the receiver with a little sigh.

'Remember those initials on the gold watch?' he asked Brook.

'Yes – A.M.M.'

'They were the initials of Miss Grant's husband. Yes, she was married, and her husband's name was Arthur Morgan Maxwell.'

'Not our Maxwell?'

'His elder brother, to whom he was devoted. He died from poison nearly five years ago, and his wife – Sophia – was arrested in Buffalo where they lived and charged with murder. There was a long drawn-out trial at which the brother – our Maxwell – gave evidence for the prosecution. He said that his brother had told him that his wife hated him and wanted a divorce which he refused to aid her in getting. Towards the end of the trial the defence produced two witnesses who swore that on the night when Maxwell must have taken the poison his wife was staying with them, and was not out of their sight for more than a few minutes. Mrs Maxwell was acquitted. She sold up her old home, travelled around for a while and finally came to England where she resumed her maiden name. I think we shall have to see Mr John Maxwell before he catches that boat and now is as good as any other time.'

Maxwell was out when they reached his hotel, but he returned after they had waited for over an hour in a corner of the lounge. He came across to them and appeared to be rather unsteady on his feet. When he spoke McLean realised he had been drinking heavily.

'Mr Maxwell,' said McLean, 'I have a few questions to ask you in connection with Miss Grant's death, but this is scarcely the place to ask them. Would you be good enough to come to Scotland Yard where we shall get privacy?'

'What a time of night to start asking questions,' hiccoughed Maxwell. 'All right, if you say so.'

In McLean's office McLean's attitude was very different.

'In your evidence you gave us to understand that Miss Grant was a complete stranger to you,' he said sternly.

'That's right.'

'Is your memory so bad that you cannot remember your brother's wife whom you saw in court four years ago when she was on trial for murder?'

The effect of this upon Maxwell was electrical. His whole frame tightened up, and his mouth opened and closed speechlessly. Finally he found his voice.

'I – I had forgotten,' he said. 'I've had a lot of business worries – a long illness, too. Yes, you're right. I can see that now.'

'Not only now,' said McLean. 'According to your evidence you never left Cummings' house from the time you arrived there until after your sister-in-law was murdered.'

'I did not. I went to the toilet...'

'You went into the garden where you knew she had gone. Quite near the place where she was murdered you lighted a pipe or cigarette. The strip matches which you used and threw away bore the name of the ship which brought you to England. You hated her, didn't you, because you were certain she had poisoned your brother? You refused to accept the finding of the jury. When you saw her again so unexpectedly all that old hate was reborn...'

'She was guilty,' Maxwell shouted. 'I

174

discovered that afterwards. The man and his wife who provided her with an alibi were heavily bribed. I saw the man when he was dying only a year ago. He told me the truth – that he committed perjury. I wanted to get a signed statement but he died before I could get it. So why…?'

He stopped suddenly as he realised that he had said far more than was good for him, and McLean knew from the terrified expression that his case was nearly at an end.

After spending a month in prison, awaiting trial, Maxwell's health went to pieces and it seemed most unlikely he would ever be brought to trial. It was then that he made a full confession.

'What does it matter now?' he asked. 'I'm a dying man and justice has been done.'

McLean was inclined to agree with him.

10

The Letter

I

Roger Arnold, solicitor, of Lincoln's Inn, signing a batch of letters, with one eye on the clock, sighed with relief as he signed the last one. He had had a frantic day, most of which had been spent in the Law Court, and now he wanted to get home before the fog outside thickened and made travel almost impossible. There was a tap on the door and his stenographer entered.

'Yes, Molly – I've finished,' he said, handing the tray of letters to her.

'Thank you, sir,' she replied. 'But I really came in to tell you that Mrs Wanborough is outside and would like to see you. She says it is very urgent.'

'What a nuisance!' said Arnold. 'She talks such a lot once she gets going, and I want to catch my train. All right, show her in.'

The girl hesitated a moment.

'Well?' asked Arnold.

'I – I think I should tell you, sir. She's behaving very strangely – as if she has been drinking.'

'I wouldn't be surprised,' said Arnold. 'Sobriety is not one of her virtues. I'll risk being abused.'

A minute later the door opened and Mrs Wanborough was ushered into the room. She was quite a beautiful woman in the early thirties, with bold dark eyes and rather pronounced cheek-bones. She seemed to stagger as she came forward.

'Good afternoon, Mrs Wanborough,' said Arnold. 'Do be seated. I'm sorry I'm rather pushed for time as I have a train to catch. What can I do for you?'

'I – I'm in great trouble. Can't explain in detail,' she hiccoughed. 'I've a letter here addressed to the Commissioner of Police. I want you to take care of it and to hand it to the police if – if anything should happen to me. Will you do that?'

She took the long, heavily sealed letter from her handbag and pushed it into Arnold's hand. He gazed at the scrawling handwriting.

'But, Mrs Wanborough,' he protested. 'If you should have reason to believe that your

177

life is in danger why not go to the police and tell them?'

She shook her head vigorously.

'I can't – not now. I could be wrong and that would cause all sorts of unpleasant enquiries. Really I know what I am doing, and I'm sure it's best this way.'

'But am I to hold this letter indefinitely?' he asked.

'Oh no. Just for a period – perhaps a month or two. Perhaps in that time I shall come along and destroy it.'

Arnold finally agreed to do what was asked of him, and Mrs Wanborough waited while he opened the safe, put the letter into a black box which he locked and replaced in the safe, locking that also.

'There you are,' he said.

She thanked him and then he saw her to the door.

Several weeks passed and Arnold saw no more of his client, but he was far from forgetting the incident, for every time he opened the safe he saw the slim black box, and cogitated on what had passed between him and the strange Mrs Wanborough. The big surprise came one morning when he arrived at the office rather earlier than usual. He produced the door-key and then discovered that the lock had been forced and that the door could be pushed open quite easily.

He hurried to the outer office to find there no sign of any disturbance. But his own room was in chaos. Every drawer in his big desk had been ransacked and documents and other items were scattered on the floor. The safe had been wrecked by some device and on the floor was the slim black box with the lid curled back like an empty sardine tin. The sealed letter had gone!

In response to his telephone call to Scotland Yard came Inspector McLean, Sergeant Brook and two men from the fingerprints department. Arnold was now able to say that nothing was missing but Mrs Wanborough's secret letter, which appeared to be the motive for the burglary.

'What do you know about that lady?' McLean asked.

'She's been a client of mine for about five years. Her husband died and left her a considerable fortune. I acted for her in the matter of probate and afterwards continued to act for her in respect of some properties which she inherited. She did some rather foolish things such as backing plays which flopped, but she did rather well on the stock market. There were no children to my knowledge and she did not marry again. What her social life was I don't know. She was inclined to tipple quite a lot, and when she handed me the letter she had clearly been drinking very hard.'

'Did she give you no hint at all of what was in her mind to cause her to write that letter?' McLean asked.

'None.'

'Where does she live?'

'Gainsford House, Kensington. Flat number six.'

After spending some time with the fingerprint men, who were not having much success, McLean and Brook drove to Gainsford House. The hall porter said he had not seen Mrs Wanborough that morning. It was far too early for her to be about. She usually went out about twelve o'clock. So McLean and Brook took the self-operating lift to the first floor, and rang the bell at No. 6. There was no reply, and a second and third ring brought the same result.

McLean was about to turn away when a woman armed with a bucket and mop approached the door. She felt in the pocket of her apron for a key and glanced at them.

'If you're going inside will you please tell Mrs Wanborough that a police officer would like to see her,' said McLean.

'Okay, but I expect she is in bed at this time.'

She left the door ajar and vanished from view. Within a minute she was back again, her eyes popping out of her head, and almost incapable of speech.

'She ... she...' she stammered.

Sensing tragedy McLean entered the place and came to an open door on the right of the hall. It revealed a large and luxuriously furnished sitting-room. Lying on a couch to the right of the fireplace, clad in a colourful boudoir gown, was a fairly young dark and beautiful woman. Her eyes were open and staring up at the ceiling. One hand was across her breast; the other hung lifelessly over the edge of the couch.

McLean went close to her and saw that the shapely throat was swollen and bruised. He felt one of the hands and found it stone cold.

'Strangled!' said Brook.

'Yes – hours ago.'

The white-faced charwoman had come to the door where she stood wringing her hands together.

'Is she Mrs Wanborough?' McLean asked.

'Yes. Oh, poor lady – poor lady!'

'Please wait in the kitchen,' said McLean. 'I'll see you in a few minutes.'

II

Brook closed the door after the departed woman, and came back to McLean, who had picked up a handbag from a chair and was examining the contents.

'Not robbery,' he said. 'Here is a bundle of bank-notes, and a gold and platinum cigarette-case. It looks as if she had good grounds for her fears, and that the guilty person knew of her visit to her solicitor and took very effective steps to destroy the letter which she left with him, before he dealt with the lady herself. Better get a doctor here, Brook.'

When the doctor arrived he made some tests and gave it as his opinion that the woman had been dead for over twelve hours, and that she had been strangled with a narrow piece of material. He ruled out a rope or cord.

'There seems to be nothing in the room

which could have done it,' he added.

'No other injuries?' McLean asked.

'There's a large bruise on her right breast. Probably that was done to reduce her resistance.'

McLean now took a very close look at the corpse. Underneath the boudoir gown she was fully dressed, but on her feet she wore slippers lined with lambswool. It was soon clear that the doctor had not been very observant, for on the face of the little gold wrist-watch was a large spot of blood, now dry.

'Where did that come from?' he asked.

The doctor stared at it.

'I didn't notice that,' he admitted. 'I'm positive there is no skin breakage anywhere.'

McLean examined the two hands, and underneath two painted nails on the same arm as the wrist-watch he found more traces of dried blood.

'There was resistance after all,' he said. 'She evidently clawed the man who murdered her while she had breath left.'

The doctor was in agreement and finally left. McLean resumed his examination of the room.

'Absolutely no sign of her visitor,' he mused. 'One tumbler, a bottle of whisky half empty, five cigarette-butts, all stained with lipstick. She certainly wasn't entertaining him.'

'But she must have let him in, unless he had a key of his own,' said Brook.

The remark was a little too obvious and McLean let it pass. He went to the bedroom which had been occupied by the dead woman. It was scrupulously tidy, except for a tailored suit and a pair of outdoor shoes which had apparently been discarded when the boudoir gown and slippers had been donned. There were many nice articles in the room which would attract a burglar, and in a drawer of the dressing chest was a casket containing some quite good jewellery.

'He seems to have come for one purpose only,' said McLean.

'What beats me is that business of the letter,' said Brook. 'She expected to be done in and must have had a pretty good idea who was after her blood. Why didn't she come to us and tell us?'

'Obviously because she had something to hide. But let's see if that charlady can help.'

They went to the kitchen where the charlady was regaling herself with cups of tea. She seemed to have recovered from her first petrifying shock.

'What's your name?' McLean asked.

'Mrs Emily Hunt. I'm a widow with two children.'

'Do you come here every day?'

'Yes – round about ten o'clock. I spend an hour here and an hour in number five.'

'So you wouldn't know much about Mrs Wanborough's friends?'

'Nothing at all. No one calls at that time of the day. Mrs Wanborough seldom got up until about half past ten.'

'What about telephone calls while you were here?'

'There were a few now and then. A gentleman named Digby sometimes telephoned. As a matter of fact he telephoned yesterday morning. But Mrs Wanborough had just gone out. I left a note to tell her that Mr Digby had telephoned and would like her to ring him up when she came in, just like the gentleman told me.'

McLean dismissed her when he was satisfied she had nothing else to tell him. The subsequent search for letters produced a few which seemed innocent enough on the surface and McLean kept them for further investigation. He consulted the telephone chart under 'D' for Digby but failed to find the name.

'The woman may have heard incorrectly,' he muttered, and started to look through the whole chart.

'This is probably it,' he said. 'Not Digby but Rigby – Mayfair 22964. Look up the telephone book and find the address.'

Brook was not long in finding this. It was a very superior address in the Park Lane area. McLean waited until the ambulance arrived to remove the body, and then he locked up the flat and proceeded to investigate Mr Rigby. He was at home when McLean rang the bell at his luxury apartment – a ruddy-faced, well-built man in the early forties. The room into which he showed his visitors had a nice collection of books and some good paintings.

'It concerns a lady named Mrs Wanborough,' said McLean. 'I believe you are a friend of hers?'

'Yes. I have known her for about two years. But is anything wrong?'

'She was murdered last night at her flat,' said McLean.

Rigby's reaction was most emotional. His ruddy face became almost pale, and his lips jittered.

'Mur-dered!' he gasped. 'Oh, no – no. I loved her. I wanted to marry her.'

'Did you see her yesterday?' McLean asked.

'Yes. I rang her up but she was out. Later she rang me back and we arranged to have lunch together.'

'At what time did you leave her?'

'About half past two. I walked back with her to her flat and left her there.'

'You say you wanted to marry her. Was she willing?'

'No – not at once. She told me she would think it over.'

'Are you in business?'

'No. Until two years ago I ran a tea plantation in Ceylon. But things weren't very comfortable there and I sold out and came to England. I had lost my wife in Ceylon ten years ago, and never thought of marrying again until I met Mrs Wanborough.'

'Did she appear to be quite normal yesterday?'

'No. She seemed very depressed. I asked her if she was quite well and she said she had been sleeping badly.'

'Did she ever tell you that she went in fear of her life?'

'Good gracious, no!'

'Do you know anything of her past life?'

'Not a great deal. I know that for some years she was governess to some English children whose father had some sort of diplomatic post in Paris. She spoke French fluently and later she got into French films. It was then that she met Wanborough and married him. I got the impression the marriage wasn't very successful. Anyway, it didn't last very long, for within two years he was dead.'

'What was her maiden name?'

'Laura Truman.'

'And you know of no reason why anyone should want to do her harm?'

'No one at all. I am completely astounded.'

'Do you know the whereabouts of any living relatives of Mrs Wanborough?'

'No. She never mentioned any relatives to me.'

McLean did not return immediately to the dead woman's flat but called on Arnold, the solicitor.

'Your men seemed to have discovered nothing of any importance,' Arnold said. 'It seems to be a particularly well-planned job. Did you see Mrs Wanborough?'

'Mrs Wanborough was strangled last night,' replied McLean. 'It was not intended that she should be free to write another letter or perhaps to speak openly.'

'Shocking!' said Arnold. 'Oh why, why didn't she go to the police in the first instance?'

'If we knew why she didn't it might help enormously,' replied McLean. 'Do you know if she made a will?'

'I'm pretty sure she didn't. When she inherited her husband's fortune I mentioned that point to her. She said there was plenty of time for that, and I heard no more about it.'

'What do you know about her late husband.'

'Precious little. He seems to have spent most of his time in foreign countries. Mad on sailing. It was that which brought about his death. His motor yacht was wrecked somewhere off Jamaica. His wife was with him at the time. They managed to get away in a small boat, but later that was wrecked. Wanborough was drowned, but his wife was picked up alive.'

'I presume they found Wanborough's body?'

'Yes.'

'What was Wanborough's home address?'

'Hartford House near Ilford. It's the old family house, but it was divided into two after the death of his father, and he occupied one part of it when he was in England, which wasn't often. The other part is occupied by his brother.'

III

McLean decided to pay a visit to Ilford and two hours later he and Sergeant Brook arrived at the big old house. There were now two separate doors into the portico, marked No 1 and No 2 respectively. McLean rang the bell at No 1, but getting no reply he rang the other bell and in a few moments a middle-aged woman came to the door.

'Is Mr Wanborough at home?' McLean asked.

'Yes, but he is unwell. I am his sister. Can I give him any message?'

'I should like to speak to him personally. I am a police officer.'

'Please come in,' she said. 'I will see if he can come downstairs.'

She left them in the sitting-room and was absent for a few minutes. When she returned she said her brother would be down at once. He entered the room shortly afterwards, clad in a dressing-gown and wearing a bandage round his forehead.

'I had the misfortune to fall off a ladder,' he explained. 'What can I do for you?'

'It concerns your sister-in-law,' said McLean. 'Did you know that she was dead?'

'Good heavens, no! I haven't heard from her for six months. What happened?'

'She was murdered at her London flat last night.'

'How shocking! What was it – burglary?'

'No. Nothing appears to be missing. It is in evidence that she went in fear of her life. Can you corroborate that?'

'No. Whenever I have seen her in the past she seemed quite happy.'

'Had she not occupied the apartment next door recently?'

'No. She hated the place after my brother's death and took that flat in London.'

'Were you here all day yesterday?'

'Yes. I did some work in the garden until it grew dark. It was then I fell off a ladder which I was using to saw a branch off a tree.'

'Was your sister at home then?'

'No. She had gone down to Southend to see a friend and didn't come home until eleven o'clock.'

'Did you call a doctor?'

'No. I didn't think it was bad enough for

that. There is only a small cut.'

McLean's suspicions were now increasing. Here was a man who might conceivably benefit from the death of his sister-in-law and who had no proof that he was at home during the time of the murder. Had he really received that head injury in the way stated? To check this he and Brook went out into the garden. There were a number of trees, but not one of them showed any sign of a saw. He then forced an entry to the adjoining apartment. It was fairly tidy and rather dusty, but there were signs that it had been used quite recently, for there were newspapers and magazines dated up to a fortnight previously.

'I think he's lying,' said McLean. 'If he's not he won't have any objection to our having a close look at his head injury.'

But later, when asked to show his injury, Wanborough had emphatic objections. McLean then asked him if he would indicate the tree from which he had sawn a branch. He became confused and said he hadn't really started to saw it when he fell. McLean merely smiled and went out to the garage where Wanborough kept his car. In one of the door pockets he came upon a long narrow strip of tough linen, and in the garage itself he found an old sun-blind from which the strip had been torn.

'The garrotte,' he said to Brook. 'But no tools which look likely to have opened that safe. But we must be satisfied with what we have.'

The next day Wanborough was taken into custody. At Scotland Yard his head bandage was removed. It revealed two long scratches down the centre of his forehead, both of which had bled. McLean was now satisfied, and Wanborough was charged with murder. Some months later he was tried and found guilty. On the following day he asked to see McLean. He was astonishingly calm.

'You win, Inspector,' he said. 'But I want to clear up one thing. I didn't kill her for gain. I killed her because I am absolutely convinced she killed my brother. He couldn't swim and she was an expert. She won prizes for long-distance swimming. When they were in that open boat I'm sure she pushed him overboard, and later took to the water herself. She tried to poison my brother a year after their marriage, but it failed. I taxed her with it but she denied it and said that if I tried anything crazy I would regret it, because she had left a sealed letter with her solicitor which would put me on the spot. Well, I made my plans to get that letter, and then finish her off. She was just a cheap gold-digger with no conscience at all. That's the whole truth.'

McLean thought a great deal about this statement, but was quite unable to make up his mind as to how much truth there was in it.

'Condemned men have been known to lie before now,' he said to Brook. 'Anyway, it makes no difference.'

11

Rosie Watkins

I

The chief attraction at the 'Mermaid' Inn at Wapping was not its ancient saloon bar, with its many interesting maritime souvenirs, nor the quality of the beer, but Rosie Watkins the barmaid. No one knew this better than Frank Osborne who owned the place, and he blessed the day when young Rosie, having lost her father on a tramp steamer at the age of seventeen, came to him and asked him for a job.

From washing up in the kitchen, Rosie graduated to part-time barmaid and in due course to full-time servant of the drinking public. She liked her customers and her customers liked her, for the passing years were kind to her appearance and she was as old Bill Mason, a retired shipmaster, was wont to say, an 'eyeful'. She knew almost everyone who came into the place and seldom had need to ask them what brand of drink they required.

Osborne was not slow to realise Rosie's value to his business, and when Rosie suggested a raise in her wages she got it without argument.

'We'd never be able to replace Rosie,' he said to his wife. 'She's one in a million. If we lost her our takings would go down with a wallop.'

'Yet we'll lose her one day,' said Mrs Osborne. 'A girl with her looks and figure isn't going to stay unmarried for life, and she's only twenty-six.'

Osborne winced at this warning of grave possibilities. But he had what he thought was a solution if the emergency arose.

'If Rosie ever contemplated marriage I'd

offer her a share in the business,' he said. 'A kind of partnership. I guess that would appeal to her.'

'When a girl's in love you can't hope to buy her off with money,' said Mrs Osborne, with a shake of her head.

'But Rosie isn't in love. I've watched her when she's in the bar. She treats all the men alike – no favours at all. I don't believe Rosie is the marrying type. She's happy here and I mean to keep her happy.'

When Christmas came Osborne was as good as his word and presented Rosie with fifty pounds in crisp five-pound notes as a bonus for her good offices, and Rosie spilt a few tears in expressing her thanks.

It was a month later that an astonishing thing happened. Every Wednesday Rosie had time off from the closing of the 'Mermaid' at two-thirty until what time it suited her to return at night. But to Osborne's amazement she did not return, nor did she send any message to explain her absence.

On the following morning Osborne communicated with the police and a young constable came along to take particulars. He was far too casual for Osborne's liking and Osborne told him so.

'Well, Mr Osborne,' he said. 'If we got all hot and bothered about a young woman who stays away from her job one night we would be in a mess. Has she any parents or relatives whom she might have visited?'

'No, she hasn't, and she's not the sort of girl you seem to think she is. Rosie's as straight as a die and has never let me down in all the nine years she has been with me. Either she has met with some accident or there's been dirty work.'

The constable said it would be easy to check the first possibility as by the time he got back to headquarters all cases of street accidents would have been reported.

'But if she should return let us know at once,' he said.

Rosie's name was not among the casualties taken to, or detained in, hospitals. Nor did the worried innkeeper hear from her either by post or telephone. But on the following evening old Captain Mason came into the bar to find a group of men discussing Rosie.

'What's all this about Rosie?' he asked.

'She disappeared two nights ago,' said a man. 'Took her usual night off and never came back. On Wednesday it was.'

Mason looked across at worried Mr

Osborne who nodded his head dejectedly.

'But I saw her on Wednesday evening,' said Mason. 'About half past seven it was, near the bottom end of Regent Street. A taxi stopped outside a restaurant and out stepped Rosie with a young fellow. Before I could catch her eye she went inside with him.'

'Are you quite sure it was Rosie?' asked Osborne.

'Of course I'm sure. She was wearing a black sort of jacket, and a silly little hat like a cockle-shell. She had a pink scarf round her neck.'

Osborne's eyes bulged for he knew that this description was correct.

'Did you know the young man?' he asked.

'Never seen him in my life. Proper dandy he was, about Rosie's own age. Surprised me quite a bit.'

Osborne was of the opinion that the police should be told without delay and he asked Mason if he would come with him to Scotland Yard. Mason was agreeable, and while Mrs Osborne looked after the bar they went off in Osborne's car.

Inspector McLean who had the case in hand saw the pair in his office. Osborne explained the situation and Mason repeated what he had told Osborne.

'Where exactly was the restaurant into which the couple went?' he asked Mason.

'On the right-hand side of Regent Street, going up from Piccadilly Circus. Not very far up.'

'Was it the Café Royal?'

'That's it,' said Mason. 'I had forgotten the name.'

'Tell me more about the man. His height, the clothes he was wearing – anything you can remember.'

Old Mason reflected for a moment.

'About five feet nine,' he said. 'On the slim side. He wore a dark suit, with a pin-stripe in it. Had a hat but was carrying it in his hand – dark grey. Oh yes, his hair was dark and crew-cut if you know what I mean.'

'I know,' said McLean. 'Clean shaven?'

'Yes. That's about all I can remember.'

McLean turned to Osborne who seemed to be deep in reflection and was twiddling his fingers.

'Does the description fit anyone who might have come into your bar and seen the girl there?' he asked.

'It didn't until my friend mentioned that crew-cut hair. Now I recall that there was a man who called in – twice I think within the last fortnight. Perhaps when I wasn't there too. But Rosie didn't seem to be interested in him. When he took off his hat I noticed the way he did his hair. Looked like an overgrown "Teddy" boy.'

'Was anyone with him on those occasions?'

'There was a big fellow – like a bruiser – but I can't be sure whether they were together, for I was very busy.'

McLean ultimately promised to do something about the matter and the pair left.

II

'I think we must accept the fact that something out of the usual has happened to the girl,' McLean said to Sergeant Brook. 'If she took it into her head to elope with her crew-cut friend there seemed no reason why she should leave Osborne in the dark, not to mention all her personal belongings at her place of employment. Run along to the Café Royal and see if you can get any information there. We've already got particulars of the woman's dress.'

Brook carried out this mission, and after being absent for an hour came back to make his report.

'The head waiter in the grill room remembers them,' he said. 'They had a full meal, with champagne, and left about nine o'clock. The woman was a complete stranger to him, but the man had been there on previous occasions. He doesn't know his name, but he is certain that on a previous visit he was with an artist named Harry Brett who has a studio in Chelsea, and who is a regular customer.'

McLean knew several artists in the Chelsea group, and after one or two telephone calls he succeeded in getting Brett's address. Half an hour later he and Brook were in Brett's studio where he was working.

'Yes, Inspector,' he said. 'The man you describe must be Burt Wayland. He's an American, and I met him on a ship coming back from New York. I've seen him a few times since then.'

'What do you know about him?'

'Not a great deal. I think his father died recently and left him a pile of dollars. He's just running around having a look at the world.'

'Do you know a young woman named Rosie Watkins?'

'No. I'm sure I don't.'

'Did Wayland ever mention her in conversation?'

'No.'

'When did you last see him?'

'About three weeks ago. I took him to the Café Royal.'

'Do you know where he lives?'

'Yes. He has a flat in Camden Crescent – number four.'

McLean thanked him, and then he and Brook drove to Camden Crescent, and rang the bell on the second floor of number four. There was no response. Later McLean and Brook tried again but with the same result. There was no one in attendance at the office on the ground floor, but McLean found a bell under which were the words 'Hall Porter'. He pushed it and a minute or two later an elderly man came up some stairs from the basement.

'I'm a police officer,' said McLean. 'Is Mr Wayland still living here?'

'Yes, but I think he's away, as I haven't seen him these past few days.'

'Have you a key to his flat?'

'Yes. I have a master key which opens all the flats.'

'Will you open up number four for me?'

The man shook his head.

'I'm sorry,' he said. 'I can't do that unless you have a warrant.'

'I only want you to look inside and tell me if everything is all right there.'

The hall porter hesitated and then nodded his head.

'No harm in that,' he said. 'I'll come up with you.'

They went up in the lift and the hall porter produced his master key. He went inside, leaving the door slightly open. There was a few moments of silence and then the man came hurrying to the door, his face lined with horror.

'He – he's dead,' he gasped. 'Murdered!'

McLean did not wait upon ceremony but passed through the door immediately, with Brook following up. In the main room the body of a handsome young man lay prone on the floor with a horrid wound in his head. By the state of the blood around him it was clear that he had been there some days. The crew-cut hair and the other physical details left little doubt that he was the wanted man.

The room was in a state of chaos. A bureau and a chest of drawers had been ransacked, and articles were strewn about the floor. In the other rooms there was similar disorder. McLean came back to the main room where the body lay. The cushions on the big couch were rumpled, and on the floor, partly concealed by the couch was a pink scarf. Brook gave a low whistle at the sight of it.

'So Rosie Watkins was here when it happened,' he said.

'It looks very much like it. Anyway, get through to headquarters and ask for an ambulance and a doctor.'

While waiting for their arrival McLean and Brook carried on with the investigation. In one of the bedrooms he found traces of face powder on the base of a mirror, which suggested that the lady visitor had gone there to powder her nose.

'It's conceivable that she was in this room titivating when the attack took place,' he said. 'I can't believe Wayland was murdered in full view of a witness. When she came back the intruder – or intruders – had a problem on hand. They had either to kill her or take her away. Apparently they decided against a double murder.'

Later the medical evidence was that Wayland had died from a single very heavy blow on his head, and that he had been dead about three days. McLean found the implement – a silver candlestick which had been bent out of shape by the impact. It was closely examined for fingerprints but without success.

In the dead man's pocket was a wallet containing a great number of dollar bills and a few English notes, which caused Brook to suggest that the motive was not gainful. But McLean was of a different opinion.

'They didn't turn out all those drawers for nothing,' he said. 'I think they were after bigger fry. Here's a passport. It gives his address as 27 East Street, Chicago. He left New York last March and since then has been in Italy and France. Arrived in England three months ago. I shall have to get through to the Chicago police.'

McLean's subsequent talk with the Chicago police elicited interesting information. Wayland was known to them as the 'Dude'. He and three other men had robbed a jeweller's shop four months previously. One of his accomplices was in prison, but the other two named Hogan and Bettany had escaped. It was believed they were all together in South America. McLean asked for full physical descriptions of Hogan and

Bettany and was told they would be sent on the night plane.

At London Airport the next morning McLean and Brook collected the urgent package. It included photographs of the two gangsters taken when they served their last prison sentence.

'The man who went to prison squealed on them,' said McLean. 'Goodness! What a couple of ruffians! I'm sorry for Rosie Watkins. Take a look at them.'

Brook scanned the photographs and nodded his head.

III

In quick time hundreds of copies of the photographs were printed and sent to police stations and ports. McLean refrained from using the press or the B.B.C. for obvious reasons, and prayed that the two men had not already managed to leave the country.

It was a police constable named Wilkins to whom the printed circular rang a bell immediately it came to hand. He stared at the bigger of the two wanted men – Hogan – and gave a little gasp.

'I'll swear I saw this fellow yesterday,' he

said to the Sergeant in charge of the station. 'I had finished duty and decided to go out in my boat and try for some fish. It was about eight o'clock in the evening. I was near the river bank when he came along, making for the village. I gave him a good evening, and he replied. He was carrying a suitcase and wearing sea-boots.'

The Sergeant stared at him.

'It's a million to one against it, Ned,' he said. 'It must have been getting dark at that time. You could easily make a mistake.'

But Wilkins was insistent and the Sergeant finally decided to report the matter to headquarters. When McLean received the information he was interested enough to take the matter up.

'Sea-boots suggests a boat,' he said. 'And the locality is favourable for anyone with a boat wanting to slip across to France. Get a car and we'll leave at once.'

Arriving at the small village along the Thames estuary McLean saw the constable. He stuck to his story.

'He wasn't the sort of fellow one could forget easily,' he said. 'Has a face like a bulldog. He was in a hurry too, and seemed a bit startled at running into me.'

'I should like you to come with us and

show us the exact spot where you saw him,' McLean said.

'Certainly, but you won't be able to take the car all the way.'

He got into the police car and then directed Brook, who was driving. After about two miles they reached a region of rushes and quagmires, and soon they had to park the car. There was a beaten track through the rushes to the stony beach, but the constable stopped short of the beach where two paths met.

'It was just here,' he said.

McLean stared over the rushes and saw the river about two hundred yards away. On the tideway were a number of vessels going in both directions. Closer to the shore was a solitary craft swinging a little on the tide. It was a cabin motor cruiser.

'Did the man come from that direction?' McLean asked, pointing to the motor cruiser.

'Yes, Inspector.'

'Was that boat there last night?'

'Yes.'

'Where do you keep your own boat?'

'Away to the right. It's only a small dinghy – drawn up above the tide mark.'

'Can you row us across to the cruiser?'

'Yes, but she won't take the three of us. When she rides low she ships water. Needs a repair job.'

'All right. Sergeant Brook can row. You wait on the beach.'

The boat was indeed a cockleshell, but McLean and Brook got aboard after dragging her into the water. Brook took the oars and they made good headway towards the cruiser. As they drew near the first thing McLean noticed was that her name *Mary Jane* had been freshly painted, while the other paintwork was most shabby.

'I want to get aboard, Brook,' he said. 'But put the dinghy on the seaward side.'

Brook did this and McLean climbed aboard. The small cabin contained two bunks and some fitted cupboards. On the central narrow table were two dirty glasses, a bottle half full of whisky and a pack of playing cards. He opened up the cupboards and found inside some clothing, two suitcases, and a pile of canned foods. The two suitcases were locked. Then he heard sounds like heavy breathing and choking. They seemed to come from behind a door, forward, which he presumed led to a wash-up and galley. But the door was locked, and there was no key visible. He called out but got no reply. Then he saw a key hanging on a hook by a porthole. He removed it and found it fitted the door. In a moment he had the door open and saw before him a young woman lying on a mattress, with her arms bound and a scarf round the lower part of her face. He removed the scarf and the tight bindings, and leaned over the half-unconscious woman.

'Miss Watkins?' he asked.

Her terrified eyes blinked at him.

'I'm a police officer,' he said. 'There's no need to worry any more. There's some whisky outside. It will do you good.'

He left her for a moment and came back with some whisky in a clean glass. Supporting her with one arm he gave her the drink. In a few minutes she was sufficiently recovered to be able to speak.

'I'm Rosie Watkins,' she said. 'I was kidnapped from the flat of a man I had met–'

'I know,' interrupted McLean. 'Did you see Wayland killed?'

'No. I was in the bathroom. I heard a noise and when I entered the sitting-room he was lying on the floor in a pool of blood. They ransacked the place and took away a leather satchel. I was brought here in a car. I'm sure they meant to drown me when they were out at sea, because I heard them talking when they were half drunk. I think they stole the boat...'

She stopped as Sergeant Brook suddenly appeared. He looked very grim.

'They're here,' he said to McLean. 'Had a small tender hidden along the beach. I've tied our dinghy close up under the bows, and they probably won't see it.'

'Good! Close that door and wait here. We'll get them when they enter the cabin.'

Time passed and then they heard the sound of oars which finally ceased. Then a voice said, 'Dump the petrol now, Bett. We'll fill the tank later. I guess it's drink time.'

'They're coming,' whispered McLean, and produced from his pocket a loaded automatic.

They heard the cabin door open, and a few moments later the clinking of a glass.

'Now!' whispered McLean.

Brook pushed the galley door open. McLean went out first with the pistol levelled.

'Don't move!' he said. 'Raise your hands – quick!'

Hogan – the bigger man – put a hand to his hip pocket, but Brook was in time to get a stranglehold on him, and to rid him of an automatic. Later McLean found the leather satchel mentioned by Rosie. It was packed with fine jewellery. When they were finally lodged in jail Bettany pleaded it was Hogan who had struck the fatal blow. Both men had trailed Wayland for months, because he had run off with all the booty. But it made no difference and they were both charged with murder.

The next time McLean saw Rosie she was serving drinks in the saloon bar of the 'Mermaid' and looking as neat and attractive as ever, but just a little more serious.

12

The Foxenden Tragedy

I

The Foxenden murder provided Inspector McLean with some knotty problems. It started with the finding of the dead body of a young man in a country lane outside the village of Foxenden late on a dismal November evening. Close to the body was a battered scooter and all the evidence of a fearful crash. From the state of the scooter the County Police came to the conclusion that it had been hit by a heavy vehicle from the rear, the driver of which could not possibly have failed to realise what he had done.

The medical evidence was that the young man had been dead two hours when he was found at nine o'clock in the evening, and that the cause of death was a broken neck and head injuries. A letter on his person gave his name as Cyril Welsh, and his address as Hill Farm, Raylings, Cumberland. Communication with the address through the Cumberland police revealed that Welsh had been a tractor driver on the farm for over two years, and was on holiday. He had left the farm the previous day, and had obviously spent one night somewhere on the road.

When Scotland Yard took over the case it looked very unpromising, for it was quite clear that the driver of the heavy vehicle had no intention of coming forward. All the bits and pieces found on the road were traced to the scooter, and there were no tyre marks of any kind.

'Plain murder,' growled the County

Inspector. 'It is a straight section of road where it occurred, and of fair width. Plenty of room for a bike and a car. The car driver must have been dead drunk or have run the young man down deliberately.'

'What do you know about the victim?' McLean asked. 'I know he was employed on a Cumberland farm and was on his way to London where he was to take a holiday, but what about his family?'

'A fellow worker has stated that Welsh told him he had no parents living, and had been brought up by an uncle, a Mr Pagiter, with whom he quarrelled so badly that finally they parted company. Unfortunately our informant does not know where Mr Pagiter can be found. But Welsh did mention that he might call on his uncle while on his way south.'

'Have you advertised for Pagiter?'

'Not yet. We have only just received this information.'

McLean and Brook then went to see the body and also the shattered scooter. They were both fearsome sights, and it was abundantly clear that the scooter had received a tremendous blow from the rear.

'No doubt about the cause,' McLean said, 'and no doubt about the character of the

214

responsible person. Now, I think we will visit the site of the incident.'

Before leaving, McLean was provided with a large-scale map of the district on which the actual spot was indicated, and here an interesting point arose. Welsh was well off the London road when he was hit. There had been no need for him to pass through Foxenden at all.

'Did he make that detour deliberately?' McLean mused. 'Or did he lose his way in the darkness? I'm inclined to think that he was carrying out his half-formed intention to call on his uncle, which suggests that Pagiter lives somewhere in the Foxenden area. We'll go into that later.'

The local Inspector accompanied them to the site where there was little to indicate that a fatal accident had taken place, except for some damage done to a hedge into which the scooter had been projected, and some sand on the road to cover the blood which had been spilled.

'There was a lot of broken glass,' said the local Inspector. 'But we removed every bit we could find, and it has since been traced to the scooter lamp. But you can see for yourself that it is a very safe section of the road – dead straight for nearly half a mile.'

McLean was in agreement, but he was not content to accept the statement that his colleagues had made a thorough search of the spot, as Brook knew he would not be, and for a full hour every inch of the ground near the actual spot was gone over. It was on the further side of the damaged hedge that McLean made an important discovery. It was a piece of metal, broken from the top of an A.A. badge.

'Well, I'm dashed!' said the local Inspector. 'One wouldn't think that could have gone clear over the hedge.'

'It may have gone through the hedge,' said McLean. 'And it certainly didn't come from the scooter, because I noticed that there was a complete badge on the scooter. Very old too. At least ten years, I should think.'

A little later when the local Inspector had gone back to police headquarters in his own car, McLean and Brook drove to Foxenden. It was a small but delectable village, with a church, and a tiny square in which there were a few shops. One of these was the local post office. Here McLean saw the postmistress and asked her if she knew anyone in the neighbourhood named Pagiter.

'I don't know the name,' she said. 'But our postal delivery only covers a small area. The local directory may help. How do you spell the name?'

'I've got it written as P-A-G-I-T-E-R, but it may not be correct.'

She turned over the pages of the directory.

'Paget,' she said. 'Three of them. Pagely, Paggerly. No, there's no Pagiter.'

McLean asked to borrow the book for a few minutes while she attended to a customer who was waiting. He went laboriously through the P's and then suddenly came upon the name James Pragiter, Shamley House, Nr Ruston.

'That's on our local map, I think,' he said. 'Look it up, Brook.'

Brook found Ruston printed in very small type.

'It's about six miles from here,' he said. 'Anyone motoring from the north would naturally come through this village to get to Ruston.'

'Good! We'll look up Mr Pragiter immediately.'

Arriving at Ruston, which was no more than a hamlet, they made enquiries, and after a few disappointments they found a man who knew the house.

'It's up on the heath,' he said. 'You cross

the bridge over the stream and bear right. Then up the hill. You pass an old windmill and about two hundred yards further on you'll see the entrance to the drive.'

McLean followed these instructions and soon found the place. It was an old, spacious house lying in a natural garden of pine trees and furze bushes. A ring at the bell brought a middle-aged woman to the door.

'Is Mr Pragiter at home?' McLean asked.

'I'll see,' she said. 'What name shall I give him?'

'Tell him we are police officers.'

She left the door open and vanished through a door at the end of the hall. In a few moments she was back again piloting them to a large sitting-room where a man of about sixty was reclining in a chair with his feet resting on a stool. Beside him was a heavy walking stick.

'Excuse me not rising, gentlemen,' he said. 'But my legs are not in very good condition.'

'That's perfectly all right,' replied McLean. 'I wanted to ask you if you have a nephew named Cyril Welsh.'

'Yes, indeed I have. He lived here until about four years ago, and then went to Canada.'

'When did you last hear from him?'

'I haven't heard from him at all. My sister, who was a widow, died when the boy was about seven years of age. He came to live with me, and I sent him to a good school. He didn't do very well there, and when I tried to get him into an office he refused to take the post that was offered. Well, the upshot was that we had a quarrel and life together became impossible. He wanted to go to Canada, so I bought him a ticket, and arranged for him to receive a capital sum there. From that day to this I have never heard a word from him, which has distressed me quite a lot.'

'Have you a photograph of him?'

'Not a separate one, but over there by the bookcase there is a photograph of him in his school cricket team, taken during his last term. He is second from the left in the front row.'

McLean went to the large photograph and recognised at once the victim of the smash. He came back to Pragiter, who was looking at him questioningly.

'I have some bad news,' McLean said. 'Your nephew was killed last night, in a car accident, only a few miles from this house.'

Pragiter stared at him incredulously.

'But – isn't he in Canada?'

'He has not been in Canada for the past two years. We have traced his address to a farm in Cumberland where he has been working as a tractor driver. He was on his way to London, but he had mentioned his intention of calling on you en route.'

'How dreadfully tragic! Was there anyone with him?'

'No. He was on a scooter. Apparently he was run down by a following car, whose driver did not report the accident.'

'The swine! I should like to have seen Cyril despite his ingratitude, for my life here has been very lonely. Do you wish me to identify him?'

'He will have to be officially identified. If you don't feel up to it perhaps there is someone else…'

'No. I'll manage, if it can be tomorrow. I shall have to hire a car as I am now unable to drive. Tell me where I must go.'

McLean gave him the requisite instructions and a little later he and Brook left and returned to police headquarters.

It was while McLean was examining the wrecked scooter that he discovered an interesting fact. Despite all the damage the

220

petrol tank, though badly battered, was still in watertight condition, and was almost full of petrol.

'He must have got a refill shortly before he was run down,' McLean mused. 'There can't be many filling stations on the latter part of his journey. If we can find the place where he bought petrol it would help to time the incident very accurately. That is rather important since the medical evidence relates to time of death, and there's no knowing how long he lived after the crash. We'll drive back on that road.'

The first three filling stations knew nothing about the scooter but the owner of the fourth one – some ten miles from the scene of the disaster had cause to remember the scooter.

'It was just before seven o'clock when the young man called,' he said. 'He wanted petrol, but while it was being put into the tank he discovered that he had a slow puncture. He asked me how long it would take to mend the puncture, and I told him it would be about twenty minutes. He agreed to have it done, and then asked me if he could use my telephone. While my assistant took over the puncture I took the young man into my office. He rang up a number and then I left him.'

'Do you remember the number?' McLean asked.

'Not the number, but it was out at Ruston.'

'Is that outside the local area?'

'Yes. It's a sixpenny call.'

'Then it will be recorded and charged to you?'

'Yes, of course.'

McLean was on the telephone himself in a matter of seconds, and within a couple of minutes he hung up the receiver.

'Thank you,' he said to the proprietor. 'That has helped a lot. Just one more question. At what time did the young man leave?'

'About half past seven. My chap had a job to get the old tyre off.'

McLean went back to the car looking enormously pleased. Brook, sitting at the wheel, looked at him questioningly.

'Revelations, Brook,' McLean said. 'That young man rang up his uncle while he was having a puncture repaired. He left this place half an hour later, and covered a distance of about ten miles when he met his fate. The crash must have taken place round about 8.20.'

Brook gave a low whistle of surprise.

'So the uncle must have known his nephew was on his way to see him?'

'That is the obvious conclusion.'

'But why did he lie?' Brook asked. 'He could have said that he was expecting the boy and that he didn't arrive.'

'Yes, but it looked safer to him to plead that he believed his nephew was in Canada. He never dreamed that we should be able to know about that telephone call.'

'Are we going back to the house?'

'No, Brook. We will leave matters until tomorrow when I am to meet him at the mortuary.'

III

But on the following morning McLean changed his mind to some extent, for instead of going straight to the place where the body lay he told Brook to drive to Pragiter's house.

'Wait in that lane up by the side of the garden,' he said. 'I think we shall be in time to see Pragiter leave in the hired car. I want to have a quick look round. We can make up time afterwards.'

Brook carried out this plan, and about ten minutes after their arrival they saw a car enter the drive, and then emerge with Pragiter inside.

'All right now,' said McLean.

The police car was driven to the house, and McLean investigated the outbuildings. There were some old stables, including a harness room which had clearly been used as a garage until quite recently for there was wet oil on the floor at just about the spot where it would drip from the sump of a car.

'Interesting,' he said. 'Now I want a word with the housekeeper.'

When questioned the woman gave her name as Mrs Giffard, and that she had been employed by Pragiter for just over three years. She was a widow.

'So you never met Mr Pragiter's nephew?' McLean asked.

'No. But he once told me he had a nephew who went farming in Canada.'

'Were you in the house at seven-thirty the night before last?' McLean asked.

'Yes.'

'Was Mr Pragiter at home then?'

'Oh yes. He had his evening meal about that time.'

'Was there not a telephone call round

about that time?'

'Yes. I answered the call. It was a man's voice. I told him I was the housekeeper and he said he would like to talk to Mr Pragiter. I went into the dining-room and told Mr Pragiter. He asked me who the caller was and I told him I didn't know. Then he went into the sitting-room to take the call.'

'What happened after that?' McLean asked.

'Nothing. He finished his meal, and went into the sitting-room. I cleared away the things, and heard the sound of the radio for a long time afterwards. I didn't see him again until I went to bed round about ten o'clock.'

This was a little bit disappointing, but not unduly so, for McLean's active mind ranged over possibilities.

'There was a car in the garage until quite recently,' he said. 'Do you know what became of it?'

'Mr Pragiter used to drive the car,' she said. 'But his arthritis got so bad he had to give up. Whenever he wanted to go anywhere he used to telephone for a hire car at Trenton's Garage in the village. He hired one this morning from there.'

McLean thanked her and then he and

Brook went to their car and drove at speed to the rendezvous. There they found Pragiter waiting in the hired car.

'Sorry to be late,' said McLean.

'That's all right,' replied Pragiter. 'We haven't had to wait long. I'll get out.'

This he did with some difficulty, and then hobbled with the aid of a walking stick to the mortuary. He nodded his head gravely as he gazed at the battered body.

'That's – my nephew,' he said. 'Poor boy!'

It was when he had climbed back into the hired car that McLean put his devastating question.

'Why did you say that you had heard nothing from your nephew in four years when in fact you had spoken to him on the telephone only an hour before he was killed?' McLean asked.

Pragiter stared at him.

'But that isn't true,' he protested. 'How can you make such an accusation?'

'Mr Pragiter, I have evidence to support that statement. At shortly after half past seven you spoke on the telephone to your nephew who intended to call on you. Do you swear that that call did not take place?'

'Of course I do – absolutely. Somebody is making a very grave error. I did speak to a man on the telephone about the time you mention, but it was not my nephew. Are you suggesting that I am in some way involved in his death?'

'I am suggesting nothing. What became of the car which until recently was in your garage?'

'I sent it to a garage to have it overhauled prior to getting rid of it.'

'What garage?' McLean insisted.

'The garage from which I hired this car. It is in Ruston village – the only garage there.'

'Thank you,' said McLean. 'I will not detain you any longer.'

The hired car went off, and after a few minutes McLean and Brook drove to the village and stopped close to the garage. Only one man was there, and he said he was Trenton the proprietor.

'I want to see the car which you removed from Mr Pragiter's garage,' said McLean.

Trenton led them to the back of the workshop where stood a big saloon car. It was quite old and had clearly been recently washed and polished. McLean went round to the bonnet, and found a dent in the near side wing, but more revealing than that was a brand new A.A. badge secured just above the heavy fender. He went to a bench which was cluttered with tools, and there found the lower portion of an old badge.

Trenton watched him nervously, but McLean said nothing until after he went to his car and found that the lower part of the badge fitted perfectly with the part that he had picked up on the site of the crash.

'Mr Trenton!' he called.

Trenton came forward, and McLean stared into his face with great intensity. It had seemed a little familiar, and now he realised why. There was a striking similarity between it and the face of Pragiter.

'When did you collect that car?' he asked.

'A week ago,' replied Trenton.

'In that case you must have used the car since, because I am certain it was the car which ran down and killed Pragiter's nephew. I believe you to be Pragiter's brother. Do you deny that?'

'Yes. My name is Trenton. I can prove–'

'I've no doubt you can, but can Mr Pragiter prove that he is really Mr Pragiter. You are under arrest. I am taking you to police headquarters. Here is your driver back again. He can carry on. Come along.'

It was at police headquarters that Trenton, under grilling questioning, broke down.

'I am guilty of a lot of things,' he said. 'But

not murder. My brother was Mr Pragiter's servant for ten years, but nearly four years ago he and my brother stayed at Exmouth where Pragiter had a sailing boat. They were caught by a storm and the boat capsized and sank. My brother managed to swim ashore but Pragiter was drowned, and his body never recovered. My brother impersonated him. It wasn't difficult because the old man was a recluse and scarcely ever went out. There were no other servants in the house. My brother then engaged a housekeeper, and he bought my silence by buying me the garage. He practised forging Pragiter's signature, and as the bank account was in London the financial side was easy. It all worked out well until that evening when my brother learned over the telephone that Pragiter's nephew was on his way to visit him. He telephoned me and told me to bring that car round, but not to come as far as the house. I waited for him and finally he joined me. You – you know the rest. I was not driving the car when it happened. He insisted on driving. There was only one road by which the boy could come. It was horrible. I – I tried to stop him, but it was no use. That's the truth – I swear it.'

The impersonator was arrested an hour later. Unlike his brother he did not panic, and to all questions he remained completely silent. McLean shook his head as finally he was taken away to a cell.

'Utterly beyond redemption,' he said.

13

House without a Mirror

I

Nobody apparently knew when Edith Chatterton left her house at Sandler's Green in North London. Her disappearance was only discovered when the police found out that it had been broken into and presumably robbed. Subsequent enquiries suggested that the woman was a bit of a mystery. She had lived the life of a recluse behind the immensely high wall which surrounded her garden, and even the postman who had delivered letters up to about three months past had never actually seen her.

At the local rates office it was learned that the last rates demand, much overdue, had not been paid. Her few neighbours in the rather remote area had seen her at a distance but never face to face. The shop-owners in the nearby village had no knowledge of her.

In due course the local police passed on the matter to Scotland Yard, and Inspector McLean went with his assistant, Sergeant Brook, to have a look at the house. They passed through an arched garden gate, and across some flagstones to the front door. A padlock had been fixed to it by the local police, and McLean opened it with the key which had been handed to him, and saw that the original lock had been forced and broken.

'It was burgled all right,' he said. 'But we have no means whatever of learning what has been taken.'

'Nor what became of the woman,' Brook added. 'It mightn't have been burglary at all, but abduction.'

In the hall there was no disturbance, but on entering the room on the right of it a bureau had been forced open, and there were other clear signs of an intruder. Upstairs only one of the bedrooms had been in use, and in this all the bedclothes were in disarray. When they had been through the whole house McLean noticed one peculiar thing about it.

'Well, that's extraordinary,' he said.

'What is?' Brook asked.

'Not a single mirror in the whole place. Can you imagine any woman living in a house with no mirror? At least you would expect to find one on her dressing-table.'

'Perhaps the burglar collected mirrors,' Brook said facetiously.

'He certainly collected smaller things, for there is a notable absence of any articles of any value. Let's try to get a picture of the woman herself. Turn out that wardrobe.'

There were a number of things which helped to compose the picture which McLean required. There were several pairs of shoes size three and a number of dresses obviously made for a very small slender woman. In the bathroom, on a hair-brush McLean found a long black hair, but nowhere a penny in cash or a bank-book of any kind.

'From the dust which has accumulated it looks as if the house has not been occupied for several months,' he said. 'There's no telephone so we can't expect any help in that direction. See if there are any old newspapers in the kitchen.'

Brook went off and was soon back with a bundle of newspapers the latest date of which was two months previously, while McLean himself had brought to light the photograph of a dark and beautiful young woman. She was wearing a short grey squirrel coat, and a hat to match, and when he compared these with two similar articles which were in the wardrobe he could find no difference.

'This appears to be the missing woman,' he said. 'But the photograph was taken by an amateur so we can't get much help in that direction, but we can get it in the press and hope for some positive results.'

The photograph appeared in several daily newspapers the next morning, along with a paragraph to the effect that the woman's name was believed to be Edith Chatterton, and that the police would be glad to hear from any person who knew the woman. By noon there were three telephone calls. Two of them were scarcely worth bothering about, but the third was much more hopeful for the caller said he was certain he had taken the photograph in the garden of an hotel at Bournemouth four years previously. He could not remember the woman's name, but was sure it wasn't Chatterton. His own address was in Putney.

'Are you speaking from your home?' McLean asked.

'No – from my office in Thames Street, Putney. My name is Thomas Creighton and I am in business with my brother, at number fourteen.'

'Will you be available in about half an hour?' McLean asked.

'Yes.'

'Then I will call on you for further information.'

McLean and Sergeant Brook left soon afterwards and had no trouble in locating the office of Creighton Bros, and were shown at once into a well-furnished office on the first floor where a comparatively young man greeted them rather excitedly. McLean who had brought the photograph with him, handed it to Creighton.

'This is much clearer than the one in the press,' he said. 'Do you still think this is the photograph you took?'

'Yes. I live only a few minutes away, and I have had time to go home and look through my negatives. Here's the one from which that print was taken.'

He produced the negative in question and McLean could see from the subject and the background that that fact was now definitely established.

'I am satisfied,' he said. 'Can you tell me the date, and the name of the hotel.'

'The hotel was "The Marlborough" and the date was between October 12th and the 26th. Nearer the former date, as I had the time to get the prints before I came home, and gave one to the woman.'

'Are you still unable to remember the woman's name?'

'Yes. It was a hyphenated name, and I've racked my brain in vain.'

'Would you recognise it if you saw it?'

'I feel sure I should.'

'I'll check that with the hotel, but in the meantime can you tell me anything about the woman?'

'She was slim and most attractive physically – dark hair and eyes and a very quiet and husky voice. She told me she came from Reading, but seemed very reluctant to talk about herself.'

'Was she still at the hotel when you left?'

'Yes. I understood she was staying for a further week.'

McLean did not detain him any longer, but on reaching Scotland Yard he got in touch with the hotel at Bournemouth and

235

asked them to look up their records and for the appropriate date and to tell him the hyphenated name of a woman whose home address was Reading. Ten minutes later he was rung back and told that a young woman named Rees-Jones appeared to be the person he was asking for. She had stayed at the hotel from the 12th October until the end of the month. Her address in the register was No 6 Minton Court, Reading.

'That's something achieved,' McLean said. 'Let's see what we can learn at Reading.'

II

Minton Court was a big comparatively new block of flats overlooking the river. It boasted a uniformed hall porter who on being questioned said he remembered Miss Rees-Jones quite well. She had occupied a flat there for two years but had given it up three years previously. He did not know where she had gone to.

'Was she engaged in any sort of business?' McLean asked.

'Not to my knowledge. She was about the place all times of the day. I think she was of independent means.'

'Do you know anything about her relatives?'

'No. There was a young man who used to visit her. He looked rather like her and might have been her brother. I remember she called him David.'

'Who are the letting agents for the flats?'

'Morgan and Morgan in the High Street.'

At the office of the agents the senior partner in the firm also remembered Miss Rees-Jones, also her brother David.

'I was very surprised when she suddenly gave up the flat,' he said. 'But I have a notion that her brother grew tired of paying the rather high rent. I don't think she herself had any money for it was the brother who always paid the rent.'

'By cheque?'

'Yes.'

'Is he older or younger than her?'

'Four or five years older I should guess.'

'Do you know where he can be found?'

'I can find his address, but that was four or five years ago.'

'I should like to have it.'

The agent delved into his file and finally found what he wanted.

'Here it is,' he said. 'The Flaxford Hotel, Marlow. I think he lived mainly in hotels. We have several old addresses – all hotels.'

'I suppose you can't remember on what bank his cheques were drawn?'

'No, I'm sorry.'

'Do you know where Miss Rees-Jones went to when she left her flat?'

'I have no idea.'

When, back at headquarters, McLean got through to the hotel at Marlow they regretted they could tell him nothing about Rees-Jones beyond the fact that he had stayed there for several months five years previously.

'It all sounds a bit queer,' Brook said, 'and we don't seem to be making very much progress. If we could find the brother we might get some useful information.'

'At least we know the woman's real name, and we'll use the press again. But before we do that it might be worth while looking up the Criminal Records. Comparatively young men who make a habit of living in hotels usually have a reason for not having a permanent address.'

Brook who was put on to that task soon came back looking very pleased with himself.

'Got him,' he said. 'He's in prison at Cardiff – at least he should be for he was charged with manslaughter five years ago and sentenced to seven years imprisonment, along with two other men. No other convictions. That's presumably why his sister used another name, and moved to that dead and alive house. Here's the dossier. Doesn't look like a thug, does he?'

McLean looked at the photograph in the dossier. It was that of a handsome dark man, very much like his younger sister, but far more heavily built. He read the accompanying details, and nodded his head.

'Get me through to the prison governor, Brook,' he said. 'We shall have to go up there.'

The report from the prison was that Rees-Jones was still there and was of excellent behaviour. Owing to this and his good education he was employed in the prison library, and seemed pleased with his work there. McLean said he wanted to question the man and would be at the prison the following morning.

The subsequent interview took place in the Governor's office. The prisoner was very neat in his appearance and perfectly composed.

'Have you a sister named Edith?' McLean asked.

'Yes.'

'Have you heard from her since you were sent to prison?'

'Only once and that was a month after I came here.'

'Where was she living at that time?'

'At the flat in Reading.'

'Have you written to her since then?'

'Yes, but my letters never reached her. They came back marked "gone away".'

'I have to tell you that your sister has been missing from a house in North London for over two months. That was only discovered recently when the house was burgled. She is not wanted on any charge, and this investigation is for the purpose of finding out if she has been the victim of foul play. Can you help us in the matter?'

The convict looked very distressed at this news, but shook his head.

'I wish I could,' he said. 'She had very little money of her own, and I made over to her all the cash I had after I was convicted.'

'How much?' McLean asked.

'Just under three thousand pounds. She had some jewellery from my mother. It might be worth a thousand pounds. I've been a fool. My father left me a tidy fortune and I squandered it. I was tempted to retrieve my

240

losses in that bank raid, but it was a dead failure. I'll tell you something which you won't believe, but it happens to be true. I never fired the bullet which killed the bank clerk. In the scuffle the pistol was dropped, but not by me. I never have owned a pistol.'

'Your two accomplices both swore the same thing.'

'I know, but if one of them did carry a pistol I wasn't aware of it. Anyway, all I got out of it was seven years, with some remission, I hope.'

'How did your sister react?' McLean asked.

'Very badly. I shouldn't be surprised if she refused to touch the money I made over to her. But it was honest money – all I had left out of my inheritance.'

'Has she any relatives or close friends to whom she might have gone?'

'Certainly no relatives, but she had one close friend – a woman who was at school with her named Winifred Tice. She is – or was a nurse at the Clayton Clinic in Paddington.'

III

When finally he was taken away McLean

241

had a talk with the prison Governor and learned from him that the two men associated with the prisoner were named George and Edward Paulding. They had served their shorter sentences at another prison and were now believed to be employed in a betting shop at Aldgate.

'We'll look them up later,' McLean said to Brook. 'But first we'll try to find Nurse Tice.'

It was on the following morning that they ascertained over the telephone that Nurse Tice was still employed at the clinic, and within a very short time they were in conversation with the very efficient-looking woman.

'Yes,' she said, 'Edith Rees-Jones is a very old friend of mine, but I haven't seen her for the past three months. Since her brother disgraced the family name she adopted her mother's maiden name.'

'Is this the woman in question?' McLean asked, and showed her the photograph.

'Yes,' she said. 'Before she had the bad accident. Such a tragedy! She was one of the most beautiful women I have ever known until then.'

'What was the accident?'

'She had a car skid on an icy road, and her

car overturned and then caught fire. She was shockingly burned about the face and arms and was in hospital for months afterwards. When she came out she buried herself away in an old house in North London, ashamed to face anyone again. Even I had trouble in seeing her.'

'That seems to account for a peculiarity about the house in question. I noticed there was not a single mirror in the place.'

'She gave me two fine old mirrors which had come from the old family house – said she never wanted to look in them again. It was all very painful to me. But why all these questions? Is she in trouble?'

'She has been missing from her home for over two months for no accountable reason.'

Miss Tice expressed her astonishment and anxiety, but added that she did not believe her friend would do anything silly despite her pessimistic outlook.

'I wish I could help you,' she said. 'But I am absolutely in the dark. But there is one thing I must tell you. Some weeks ago a woman rang me up. She said she was a very old friend of Edith's and asked me if I could tell how she could get in touch with her. I gave her the address.'

'Did she give you any name?'

'No. But she had a Welsh accent, and I knew that Edith had Welsh blood.'

Finally McLean thanked her for her information and then went in quest of the Paulding brothers. He found George Paulding after many enquiries, as the betting shop traded under another name and George was merely a clerk there. He was a furtive-looking fellow and looked a little uneasy when he knew that his visitors came from Scotland Yard.

'I've done my stretch,' he said. 'Isn't that the end of it? I'm trying to earn an honest living.'

'I'm glad to hear it,' McLean said. 'Do you live here?'

'Yes. I've a couple of rooms upstairs.'

'And your brother – did he get a job here?'

'No. Mr Grierson who runs the business had only one vacancy. My brother is somewhere up north. I haven't heard from him for over three months.'

'Didn't he give you any address?'

'No – just a postcard. It was postmarked Liverpool.'

'Did you ever meet the sister of David Rees-Jones?'

'No. I knew he had a sister, but I've never seen her.'

They were interrupted by the arrival of a portly man who looked very prosperous. He nodded to the clerk and then disappeared into a side office.

'Mr Grierson?' McLean asked.

'Yes,' Paulding said.

'Tell him I would like to see him.'

Paulding did this and McLean and Brook entered the other office. Grierson, lighting a huge cigar, nodded to him.

'How can I help you, Inspector?' he asked. 'If it concerns Paulding I must tell you I know all about his past. I gave him a job and he's holding it down pretty well.'

'Did you ever meet his brother?' McLean asked.

'Yes. He wanted a job too when I opened up the shop, but I didn't like the look of him. He comes here sometimes to see George. A very tough customer. He and his wife live in an old shack down by the river at Mortlake. What he does for a living I don't know and wouldn't care to guess.'

'Whereabouts is this shack?'

'A place called Smuggler's Lane. It's scheduled for demolition.'

McLean thanked him and went back with Brook to the police car.

'Mortlake?' Brook asked.

'Yes. Paulding must have had good reason for lying about his brother's whereabouts. Do you know Smuggler's Lane?'

'I think so.'

They found the place after some little trouble, and when McLean rang the bell at the dilapidated building a swarthy young woman came to the door.

'I am a police officer,' McLean said. 'Are you Mrs Paulding?'

'Yes.'

'Is your husband at home?'

'No. But can I help you?' she asked with an obvious Welsh lilt in her voice.

'Do you know a young woman named Edith Rees-Jones?' McLean asked.

'No,' she said.

Unfortunately for her at that moment a man appeared on the staircase behind her. She turned her head for a moment and then made to close the door, but McLean's foot prevented this. Her face grew crimson with embarrassment.

'Better – better come in,' she stammered. 'He's my husband. I thought he had gone out.'

McLean waved them both into a room on the left of the hall and then faced the glowering man.

'I believe you to be concerned in the disappearance of Edith Rees-Jones,' he said. 'I am going to take you into custody for further questioning. If you're wise you'll tell me where she is now.'

Paulding scowled, but an appealing gesture from his wife caused him to have second thoughts.

'She's upstairs,' he growled. 'In the attic. The key is on the outside of the door.'

'Look after them, Brook,' McLean said, and hurried up the two flights of stairs to the locked room. Inside he found a terribly scarred woman lying on a bed. Despite her facial injuries he was able to recognise her.

'I am a police officer,' he said. 'Were you kidnapped by those two persons downstairs?'

'Yes.'

'Why?'

'They told me that they knew I was holding some money which my brother had taken from a bank. They searched the house and then brought me here – said they would hold me until I told them where the money was.'

'Have they ill-treated you?'

'No.'

McLean brought her downstairs, and put

her in the car while he made a closer search of the house. In a drawer he found a post office savings book in the name of Edith Rees-Jones. It was then that the truth emerged. During the past month there had been withdrawal of money every few days from different post offices and always for amounts just below the limit without having to deposit the book. McLean rejoined the dejected couple.

'Someone had to forge Miss Rees-Jones's signature,' he said, 'and it must have been a woman. Was it you, Mrs Paulding?'

'Yes,' she said. 'We were desperately hard up when my husband came out of prison, and couldn't get a job.'

'Hadn't your brother-in-law a hand in this business?'

'No. Just Ted and I. We offered to rope him in but he wouldn't play. We had to hold the girl while we were using her bank-book. Now let's go. I shan't be sorry to get out of this dump.'

14

Fellow Passengers

I

Inspector McLean could not but be interested in the two Teddy boys who barged into his compartment on a slow train from Portsmouth to London. They were dressed exactly alike – black stove-pipe trousers, skin tight purple shirts under a long Edwardian jacket, richly ornamented on the lapels with gold and silver thread, and brown crêpe shoes with inch-thick soles.

Until they arrived all was peace and quiet. McLean had been alone and enjoying a book. Now they sprawled in the opposite seat, with their feet resting on the cushions on his side, and unpleasantly close to him, deliberately wiping the soles of their shoes on the clean new cushions. McLean stared hard from their shoes to their insolent faces. The shorter and broader one stared back.

'Seen enough, guvner?' he demanded.

'I've seen more than enough. Take your filthy feet off that cushion.'

'Or what?' asked the taller lout, beetling his brows. 'Watch your step, mister, or you might get hurt.'

McLean closed his book and laid it beside him.

'And what would you use to put that threat into effect?' he asked. 'Knuckle-dusters, a flick-knife, or just an ordinary cosh?'

'Aw – leave him alone, Ted,' said the short lout. 'He wasn't brought up right.'

But the thin-lipped Ted wasn't to be pacified so easily. Deliberately he moved his dirty shoe to the right and actually soiled McLean's trousers. McLean's riposte was instantaneous. He brought his knuckles smartly against Ted's exposed ankle, causing him to utter a wail of pain. But the next moment he was on his feet, limping but ferociously aggressive.

'Listen!' snapped McLean. 'If you start any trouble here I'll give you the biggest hiding you ever had.'

It was perhaps fortunate at that moment that the ticket inspector slid back the door and took in the situation.

'Hey, what's happening here?' he asked.

'See for yourself,' said McLean, and pointed to the mud-bespattered cushion and his own soiled garment.

The inspector looked at the two louts – a long look of scorn and contempt.

'Nice way to behave, I don't think,' he said. 'I could get you charged for this. Where are your tickets? Come on!'

They each produced a ticket and the inspector glared as he saw the colour.

'Travelling first on a third class ticket,' he snorted. 'You've got a nerve. Beat it, quick, or I'll hand you over to the police at the next stop.'

Scowling, they went, giving McLean a baleful glance as they passed him.

'Scum, sir,' the inspector said, as he punched McLean's ticket. 'If they were my sons I'd have licked the pants off them long before this. I don't know what this country is coming to.'

It appeared to be but an isolated incident in McLean's busy life, but it didn't work out that way, for about six months later a police constable, on a late 'beat' at Peckham, saw some bloodstains on a pavement. He was able to follow them up, for they were still wet, and his quest led him to a builder's

251

yard. Inside this was the body of a young man. He was in full Teddy-boy kit, and was marked by many knife wounds, but the medical evidence was that none of these injuries were of a serious nature, and that he had died from a heavy blow on the left temple, at approximately eleven o'clock that evening – half an hour before he was found by the constable.

There was nothing on his person to give his identity, but the next morning a woman named Mrs Dugwell notified the local police station that her son, Alan, was missing. She was taken to the mortuary where the body lay and there identified him as her son.

Just before this identification had taken place McLean had received a photograph of the corpse, and it sent his mind careering back to the day in the train, and his encounter with the two Teddy-boys.

'I think I know this fellow,' he said to Sergeant Brook. 'He looks very much like the shorter of those two young thugs. I believe I told you about them?'

'You did, Inspector,' said Brook. 'Do we do anything about it?'

'We do if the Chief is agreeable. I'll have a word with him.'

McLean got the case, and before he could

leave information came through to the effect that the dead man had been identified. It made the situation easier but McLean still carried out his plan to see the body first, before taking evidence, and half an hour later he was satisfied.

'It's the same man,' he told the doctor. 'I understand that you time the actual death as eleven o'clock. Would he have survived his injuries for very long?'

'In my opinion about half an hour. It was the head injury which killed him. The knife wounds are superficial.'

McLean then went to the spot where the body had been found. There were signs on the ground that a fierce fight had taken place and it was significant that at the time the gate to the yard had been padlocked.

'Evidently they climbed over the wall,' McLean said to Brook. 'When the fight was over the survivor escaped over the wall and must himself have been injured, for it was his blood that the constable saw on the pavement. Well, let's see what the dead man's mother has to say about it.'

They found Mrs Dugwell at her semi-detached house about a mile distant. She was pallid and distraught, and spoke like a well-educated woman.

'I've been a widow since 1943,' she said. 'When my husband was killed in Burma. I've had to go out to work since then to make ends meet. My son Alan has always been a problem.'

'Tell me about last night,' said McLean. 'When did you last see him?'

'At half past seven. He works in a garage – Eastmans in West Street. He came home at six o'clock, and had a meal at a quarter to seven. Then he changed his clothes and went out. He didn't say where he was going.'

'Did you object to him wearing those peculiar clothes?'

'Not then. He knew I objected, but it was no use. What could I do about it?'

'Did you know he had a flick-knife?'

'I didn't know he had one last night, but I have seen one in his bedroom.'

'Did you know his friend – a tall man named Ted?'

'No. He never mentioned his friends to me. That's what worried me. He never confided in me at all. I never knew what he was doing.'

'Has he ever been in trouble?'

Mrs Dugwell nodded her head sadly.

'Several times in the Juvenile Court,' she

said. 'But only for damaging property.'

II

It was at the garage where Dugwell had worked that McLean got a little useful information.

'I only kept him on because I had a respect for his mother,' the garage proprietor said. 'She's a fine woman, and her husband was a grand chap. The lad got right out of hand years ago. He got roped in with a wild gang – some of them potential criminals.'

'He had a companion named Ted – a bit older than himself and taller. Do you happen to know him?'

'No. I know he was often seen with a gang of Teddy-boys, but I don't know any of them. But there's a girl I've seen him with once or twice. She works in that newspaper shop up the street. I don't know her name. Flighty bit of goods if you ask me.'

The girl, when questioned, looked scared. She said her name was Grace Dilham. She was eighteen years of age, and lived with her aunt, as both her parents were dead.

'Were you walking out with Alan Dugwell?' McLean asked.

'Not regular. Sometimes I went to the flicks with him.'

'Did you see him yesterday?'

She hesitated for so long that McLean took her up.

'Look!' he said. 'This is a case of murder so don't start thinking up some lie. Did you see Dugwell last evening?'

'Yes. I went to the Regal cinema with him. But I don't know what happened afterwards, straight I don't. We – we came out just after ten o'clock and … and…'

'Go on,' said McLean.

'There were three Teddies waiting on the corner. They told me to beat it, and I didn't like the look of things so I went.'

'Why didn't you like the look of things?'

'They – they had got hold of Alan and were leading him away.'

'Did you know these three men?'

'No.'

'Think again,' said McLean sternly. 'I'm sure you're not telling the truth. Was there by any chance a man named Ted?'

'Yes,' she admitted, with a half sob. 'But I didn't know the other two.'

'What is Ted's surname?'

'Summers.'

'And what had he against Dugwell?'

'I – I don't know.'

'Was it perchance you? Had you been going about with Summers until you met Dugwell?'

Here she failed to meet McLean's gaze and broke into real tears.

'I had called it off with Ted,' she sobbed. 'I didn't like his ways. But he told me it wasn't off, and that I was still his girl. He asked me if there was anyone else and I told him it had nothing to do with him. But I don't know what happened after the cinema. I swear I don't. I went straight home. My aunt will tell you I was indoors by twenty past ten.'

'Where does Summers live?' McLean asked.

'Somewhere in Stanton Road. I don't know the number.'

'Do you know where he works?'

'No.'

McLean had no difficulty in finding the house in question. The son was not at home but his mother was. She like Alan Dugwell's mother was a widow, but of a very different type.

'Ted's out,' she said. 'Looking for a job. What's he done now?'

'I don't suggest he has done anything. I

want to question him about his movements last evening. At what time did he come home?'

'I don't know. I wasn't in when he came home. But he was here at half past ten.'

'Are you prepared to swear to that?' McLean asked.

'Well, it might have been a bit later.'

'Was he injured?'

Mrs Summers was excused from answering that question by the sudden arrival of her son. He was now dressed conventionally and seemed to be limping. He took one look at McLean's face and gasped.

'I thought you might remember me,' McLean said. 'Six months ago we met in rather different circumstances. The man who was with you on that occasion is now dead. Can you tell me anything about that?'

'No,' said Summers. 'I've only just heard about it.'

'But you were with him last night – shortly before he was killed.'

'Who says so?' Summers demanded.

'Never mind who says so. Do you deny it?'

Summers reflected for a moment. He was looking strained and curiously limp.

'No,' he said. 'I saw him for a few minutes,

and then we parted. He was all right then.'

'You were wearing your Teddy-boy clothes. I should like to see those clothes. Where are they?'

Summers looked very sick and muttered something unintelligible. His mother too was unhelpful so McLean went upstairs, and very soon found the suit, hidden under some underclothing in a drawer. With it was a flick-knife and a murderous-looking cosh. The right sleeve of the long coat was jagged in several places and around the jags was dried blood. There was also a jag in the front part. He took the items downstairs and spread them out on the table.

'Now,' he said to Summers. 'Explain these.'

Mrs Summers looked terrified.

'I – I didn't know,' she said. 'He wasn't wearing that suit when I came home last night.'

'Out with it, Summers!' McLean snapped. 'You had a fight with Dugwell last night, didn't you?'

'Yes. He was running around with my girl. We – we fought it out with knives. But I didn't hurt him much. I can show you where he stuck me – four times. At last he fell down and I left him there and climbed over the wall.'

'After you had knocked him cold with that cosh.'

'No. I never took it with me. I only had the knife. I swear I never killed him.'

'I am going to take you into custody,' said McLean. 'Are you going to come quietly, or do I have to handcuff you?'

'No – I'll come,' said Summers, almost in tears.

At the police station Summers' injuries were examined. They were not deep wounds and all of them were covered with plaster. On his right leg was a tremendous bruise which had caused him to limp.

'He kicked me there,' he said.

'Were there any witnesses to that fight?' McLean asked.

'No, sir. I sent my two pals away. You – you don't think I killed him, do you?'

'What I think doesn't matter. It's what the jury may think. You're in a bad spot, my lad, and you had better get used to that idea – and say your prayers. Now I want the names of those two other boys.'

The names and addresses were given and Summers was then lodged in a cell.

III

The other two Teddy-boys when questioned swore that Summers had only the knife as lethal weapon, but it seemed a little significant that although they had wanted to see the fight Summers had ordered them to 'beat it'.

'We'll take another look at that yard,' said McLean. 'It may provide further information.'

The constable on duty at the builder's yard let them in, and informed McLean that the owner of the yard had been worrying him about the removal of certain material. He had, of course, refused to allow it.

'Quite right,' said McLean, and then commenced his search.

The stores were of the heavy type, from joists to concrete mixers, but there was a brick building in the corner of the yard in which smaller and more removable things were housed. This was provided with a heavy padlock, but on close inspection the lock was found to be broken, and McLean was about to enter the place when the constable came to him.

'The company's work's foreman is here, Inspector,' he said. 'He wants permission to take some tools away. Says it's holding up an urgent job.'

'Let him come in,' McLean said.

The man came forward, and explained the situation. All he wanted was two planes and an electric drill which were kept inside the store. Then suddenly he noticed the broken padlock.

'You didn't do that, Inspector?' he asked.

'No. I found it that way. It looks as if the store has been burgled.'

They all entered the room. There were plenty of useful and valuable tools on shelves and benches, and the foreman's gaze took them in.

'Nothing...' he commenced, and then stared under one of the benches. 'My goodness, you're right. All our stock of lead pipe has gone, and the sheet copper. Must have been a couple of men and a lorry to have shifted that lot. Four hundred quid's worth at least. Nice of them to leave us a souvenir...'

He was about to pick up a short length of lead pipe when McLean stopped him, and retrieved the piece himself, holding it dead in the centre. At one end of it was blood.

'All right,' said McLean. 'Take the tools you want, and leave the rest to us.'

'What's it mean?' asked Brook when they were alone.

'I think it means that young Summers spoke the truth for once. As soon as I saw that cosh I doubted whether it could have caused the injury from which Dugwell died.'

'But couldn't he have broken in here...?'

'No, Brook. It doesn't make sense. What does make sense is that the place was burgled immediately after Summers left. Dugwell was a bit slow climbing over that wall, and the thieves caught him here. He probably recognised them, and they him, and that fact sealed his doom. I want this piece of pipe examined for possible fingerprints, and then I want to see Summers again.'

A few hours behind iron bars were enough to reduce Summers to a nervous wreck.

'I didn't do it – I didn't – I didn't!' he protested as soon as he came face to face with McLean.

'Perhaps we might be able to prove you didn't,' said McLean. 'Now listen. When you clambered over that wall did you see anyone in that back street?'

'No. It's a dead end.'

'What about the entrance to it. Did you see a lorry or a big car?'

'Yes. Not in the street itself, but just round the corner.'

'What sort of a vehicle was it?'

'An open lorry. I knew the chap who was in the cab. He runs a couple of lorries and does contract work for builders. He didn't see me and I didn't want him to.'

'Who is he?'

'His name is Random, but I don't know where he lives.'

It didn't take McLean long to get that information, and within an hour Random and two other men were arrested. McLean was a little disappointed when he heard that the lead pipe, which was proved to have caused the fatal injury, carried no fingerprints, but that was no longer of prime importance for hidden in the garage where Random kept his lorries was all the stolen material, and in Random's home was found a copy of the key which fitted the main gate to the builder's yard, and which was essential to the plan.

Later McLean saw Summers again. He looked even worse than on the previous occasion, for now he had spent a whole night brooding over awful possibilities.

'Summers,' said McLean. 'You are now going to be charged.'

'Tell me, sir,' he begged. 'What – what will it be?'

'What do you expect?'

Summers shook his head miserably, and tears welled up in his eyes. McLean then showed a little compassion.

'Cheer up!' he said. 'You'll get what you deserve, but no more. Another man has already been charged with the murder. You will be out of circulation for a period. Now come with me.'

15

Sonata in C

I

The pianoforte music from the next-door apartment ended in a vast crescendo and two tremendous chords which seemed to shake the whole house, and Mrs Winterton laid down her knitting and gave a little sigh.

'Thank goodness that's over,' she said. 'Now perhaps I shall be able to finish my book.'

Her husband, a retired civil servant, laughed as he stretched out his legs and knocked out his pipe on the fender.

'If you will take in professional musicians you must expect them to practise, Emily,' he said. 'As a matter of fact I rather enjoyed it.'

'Well, I didn't,' retorted his wife. 'When he took the apartment it was understood that he wouldn't practise after nine o'clock in the evening, and now it's half past. I think I shall have to talk to him about it.'

'I shouldn't,' said Winterton. 'He might take umbrage and walk out on you. Then you'd have to start advertising all over again. At least he plays good music. You might get someone who has a passion for Rock and Roll round about midnight, and holds drunken parties until the early hours. The trouble is our walls are not thick enough.'

Mrs Winterton was far from mollified. Actually she hated the whole idea of divided houses, but economic pressure had forced it upon her.

It was on the following morning that the postman arrived with a registered letter, addressed to Pierre Lescaut. He apologised for troubling Mrs Winterton, but he had to get a signature for the letter and Mr Lescaut appeared to be out.

'Oh, but he can't be – not at eight o'clock,' said Mrs Winterton. 'Perhaps the bell has gone wrong. Let me try.'

She passed across to the door which gave access to the maisonette, and pushed the bell. It was in order for she could hear it ringing loudly inside. She waited a few moments and then turned to the postman.

'You must be right,' she said. 'Is it in order for me to sign?'

'Not really, but as it's marked "urgent" I think he would like to have it.'

'All right. I'll give it to him as soon as I see him.'

She signed the slip and took the letter into the room where her husband was starting breakfast.

'What was that all about?' he asked.

'Registered letter for Lescaut. He appears to be out so I signed for it.'

'You shouldn't have done it, Emily,' he protested.

'Rubbish! That's what's wrong with you, Edmund – too much red tape. Forty years of it. Lescaut will be glad. It will save him going to the post office or waiting until tomorrow morning. Pass the coffee, dear.'

Mrs Winterton tried the next door-bell twice during the day, but there was no response, but it was not until the following morning that she became really anxious when again she rang the bell and got no response.

'He could be ill – too ill to answer the bell,' she mused. 'Do you think we ought to go in? We have that spare key?'

Winterton didn't like the idea very much but finally he gave way and together they entered the apartment. Downstairs it was very neat and tidy, but upstairs – in the room which Lescaut used for his practice – it was a very different story. Lescaut, dressed in a black velvet coat, lay beside the grand piano, with a horrible wound in his chest and blood all around him. Mrs Winterton all but fainted at the sight of the tragedy and her husband hustled her from the room and went to the telephone.

Within a very short time Inspector McLean, Sergeant Brook and a doctor were at the house, which was situated on the outskirts of St John's Wood. It was of Victorian vintage, standing in nice grounds of about an acre. They were received by Mr Winterton, and conducted to the room where the body lay. After a glance at the corpse McLean left the doctor to do his work, and took Winterton to another room for questioning.

'What is the man's name?' he asked.

'Pierre Lescaut. I think his home is in Lyons. He came to us a year ago, immediately after we had the house converted into two apartments. The furniture is my wife's, but the piano is his own.'

'Was he in business here?'

'He was a professional pianist. I think he studied in Paris and came here in the hope of building up a reputation.'

'Has he had any engagements?'

'A few, I think, but he spent an enormous time practising, and composing. He was a charming man but not very informative.'

'When did you last see him alive?'

'The day before yesterday – about five o'clock. He came back in a taxi. I was in the garden and he waved a hand to me. He spent the whole evening at the piano. Unfortunately our walls are not very soundproof and we hear it. He went on rather longer than usual to my wife's annoyance.'

'When did he finish playing?'

'At half past nine. Yesterday a registered letter arrived for him. The postman couldn't get any response so my wife signed for it. This morning we got a little anxious, thinking he might be ill. So we used our spare key and entered the apartment. My wife is still suffering from the shock.'

'Have you got that letter with you?' McLean asked.

'Yes, I thought you would wish to see it.'

He produced the fat envelope and McLean saw that it was postmarked 'Hounslow'. He opened it and drew forth ten five-pound notes. With them was a short letter from an address at Hounslow. McLean read it.

My Dear Pierre,

Of course I am happy to oblige you. Glad to hear the concert went off well. I cursed the bad luck which prevented me from attending. Do come and see me when you get a chance.

Doris

'A loan apparently,' mused McLean. 'Did he pay his rent promptly, Mr Winterton?'

'Very promptly. There is a quarter's rent due today. It is just that amount.'

McLean nodded and after a few more questions he told Winterton he would see him again later. He and Sergeant Brook then went back to the music room where the doctor was making some notes in his casebook.

'Stabbed to the heart with a long thin

270

blade,' he said. 'He must have died in half an hour at most.'

'And the time of death?'

'Difficult to say with any accuracy, but at least thirty hours.'

'There is evidence to suggest that it was after nine-thirty on Wednesday night.'

'Yes, I agree with that. Well, that's all I can do at the moment. Want to go through his clothing before he is taken away?'

McLean said he did, and quickly went through the clothing. There was nothing in the pockets except some loose cash, a bunch of keys, a cigarette-case and a lighter.

II

With the doctor gone and the body removed McLean began to examine the room thoroughly. There were stacks of music beside the piano, mostly of a classical nature, and on the music rest itself was a volume of Schumann open at the end of a pianoforte concerto. To the left was a table on which there was some manuscript – part of an unfinished composition, and near this half a dozen brand new copies of sheet music. The latter bore the title of *Sonata in*

C by Pierre Lescaut.

'One of his own compositions,' said McLean. 'These I presume are his complimentary copies.' He opened one of the copies and scanned the music. 'Quite formidable-looking stuff. Make a note of the publisher's address. He may be able to help us.'

To the right of the piano was a large radiogram of the latest type, and in a space at the bottom of it were many volumes of records, the majority of them pianoforte music of the long-playing variety.

Nowhere, except on the very site of the murder, was there any sign of blood, nor any noticeable disturbance. There were several cigarette-butts in ash-trays but all were of the same brand as those in the case taken from the dead man's clothing. McLean turned out a waste-paper basket but found in it only some torn-up bits of manuscript.

After a long time McLean had to admit that there was nothing in the room which helped the investigation in the least, and he proceeded to go over the rest of the apartment. In the kitchen he found some unwashed crockery, but the various items pointed only to one person having eaten. In the main bedroom the bed was made up, and over a chair was draped a jacket which corresponded with the trousers which Lescaut had been wearing. In a side pocket was a stamped letter addressed to Paul Severac, Bowyers Hotel, Knightsbridge. McLean opened it and found that the text was in French. He translated it for Brook's benefit.

Dear Paul,

So you are in London! I should like to see you to talk over old times but I'm afraid it is impossible as I am leaving here at once on a northern tour. What a pity it should happen this way. But now that I have your Paris address I may pop over and see you very soon as I have some business to attend to in Paris.

Affectionately, Pierre

'We should attend to this at once,' said McLean. 'Before Severac goes back to France.'

Half an hour later they were at the small hotel. McLean asked to see Mr Severac and a few minutes later he came into the sitting-room where McLean and Brook were waiting. He was a small dapper little man, with a marvellous head of curly black hair, and McLean was relieved when he spoke in broken English. He was handed the opened letter, which he read, and then stared at McLean.

'I regret that I was compelled to open it,' said McLean. 'Mr Lescaut was killed last night in his apartment. This letter was found in his coat pocket, presumably he meant to post it at the first opportunity.'

'That ees ter-rible,' said Severac. 'I get zee address from ees music publisher and hope to call on him.'

'Did you come to London especially to see him?'

'Oh no – just a holiday. Ziss is my first visit.'

'You knew him in the past?'

'Yes, for many years. But I hear nothing from him since he come to London over a year ago.'

'Was he a man who might have had enemies?'

'Who can say? He was – how you call it – rather secretive. Never telling you much about his friends or his thoughts. But he was ver' clever at music.'

'Then you can tell us nothing which might possibly help the investigation?'

'No. I hear from his family that he is doing well in London, but zat is all.'

274

'Was he partly dependent upon them?'

'I tink so, but they do not admit it.'

'How long shall you be staying here?'

'Two days more then I fly back to Paris.'

The interview was somewhat disappointing, but not unexpectedly so. McLean thanked him and then decided to go on to Hounslow to the woman who signed herself 'Doris'. He found the house and learnt that her name was Mrs Doris Sloane – a widow. They waited in a room until the lady herself appeared. She was not more than thirty and was quite charming.

'Yes, I sent him the money,' she said. 'But why this police enquiry?'

'He was murdered before your letter arrived.'

She stared incredulously and then her eyes filled with tears, and she hurriedly found a handkerchief.

'Poor Paul!' she said. 'So gifted too. I met him in Paris when my husband was alive. He was then studying at the Conservatoire. He told me that his people at Lyons were making sacrifices to give him the best musical education. I lent him the money because his rent was due and the quarterly cheque which he received from home had not arrived.'

'Was there any reason why it should be in cash?' McLean asked.

'Yes. He was overdrawn at his bank, and if he had paid a cheque into the bank it would have been placed against the overdraft. That was quite understandable.'

'Yes, of course. Did you know any of his Paris friends?'

'Quite a number. We kept rather an open house there, and both I and my husband loved music. There was a brilliant violinist named Godski, a girl who played the harp divinely, another man named Severac...'

'Paul Severac?' asked McLean.

'Yes. He was clever at improvisations. He would turn comic songs into classical sonatas.'

'Was he a great friend of Lescaut?'

'Yes, but I think he was a little jealous of Pierre being the star turn.'

'Did they ever quarrel over anything?'

'Not quarrel – just banter. All very good-natured.'

Finally McLean left the house with his mind very occupied.

'It wouldn't be a bad idea to find out just what Severac was doing from half past nine onwards,' he said to Brook.

'You want to go back to the hotel, sir?'

276

'Yes.'

Severac when questioned about his movements looked a little surprised – even resentful.

'I dine here at eight-thirty,' he said. 'I am here until about nine-thirty. Then I go into the lounge and am asked to play Bridge with three people I have met here. Major and Mrs Wren and a Miss Lovat. I go to bed at midnight.'

It took McLean but a few minutes to find out that this statement was absolutely true.

'Out goes Mr Severac!' said Brook.

III

They were back again at the scene of the crime, going through correspondence. There was reference to several concerts which Lescaut had given. A letter from his music publisher enclosing a few press notices of the Sonata in C all very favourable to the composer. Some letters from the dead man's family all full of admiration and affection, but nothing which really helped.

McLean wandered over the music room. Rather casually he opened the lid of the radiogram. He found a long-playing record

277

on the turntable, and noticed that the switch indicated 'Records'. He pushed a button and the mechanism began to work. Out of the instrument came the strains of pianoforte music, superbly played, but quite deafening.

'My goodness!' said Brook. 'That's a bit loud.'

McLean paid no attention for a few moments, and then he suddenly stopped the machine altogether. The pick-up swung away and the turntable came to rest. Carefully he removed the record and took it into a better light. The red label showed it to be Chopin's Pianoforte 'Studies' played by a world-famed pianist, but on the outside edge, just where a person would hold it to place it on the machine was a discolouration.

'Blood!' he ejaculated. 'Now we are, indeed, getting somewhere. Go next door and ask Mr Winterton if he will come here.'

McLean scarcely had time to put the record back on the machine when Winterton entered with Brook.

'Have you any knowledge of music, Mr Winterton?' McLean asked.

'Yes – if it's good music.'

'You have said that on the night of the murder you heard the piano being played

278

up to nine-thirty?'

'That is so.'

'Can you remember what was being played – towards the end?'

'I think it was Chopin.'

'I want you to listen to this record. I'll play only the end part.'

He set the machine working and dropped the pick-up quite near the end of the record. Winterton immediately looked at McLean and nodded his head. After the record had run for a minute or two the end was reached and the arm swung back, the machine automatically switching itself off.

'That was it,' said Winterton. 'Of course I thought it was Lescaut playing it on the piano.'

'That is exactly what the murderer wanted you to think,' said McLean. 'Would you agree that the music which you heard earlier in the evening was nothing near as loud?'

'Yes. At first it was quite soft, and we only heard it at intervals. Does – does it mean that Lescaut was already dead when we heard that?'

'I think there is no doubt about that. Thank you very much, Mr Winterton. Now perhaps we shall be able to make some progress.'

McLean locked up the apartment a few minutes later and hurried back to headquarters with the record. The laboratory got to work quickly. The foreign material on the record was soon proved to be blood, about two days old, but the pick-up needle travelling over it had ruined any fingerprints which might have been there.

'Never mind,' said McLean to Brook. 'It brings us back to Severac. That alibi of his is no longer effective. What we need to know is where he was between seven and eight o'clock. But first we'll go to that music publisher who gave Severac Lescaut's address.'

The publisher when questioned remembered the man who had called on him.

'He didn't actually give a name,' he said. 'He told me he was an old friend of Lescaut on a flying visit to London, and wanted to pay his respects.'

'Did he say how he knew that you had recently published a musical work by Lescaut?'

'Yes. He said he bought a copy in Paris.'

'Did he display any kind of emotion?' McLean asked.

'I thought he was rather grim. I asked him if he liked the new sonata, but he didn't reply, and went off very quickly.'

'Doesn't help very much,' said Brook when they were back in the car.

'No, but it suggests that Severac was under some strain. It was natural enough that he should want to see his old friend, but clearly the old friend didn't want to see him. There must be a reason for that, and that reason might well be the motive for murder. Now we'll see Severac again.'

When, on arriving at the hotel, McLean asked if Severac was in the receptionist stared through the door at a waiting taxi.

'I think that's his taxi,' she said. 'He is just leaving. Oh, here is the porter with his baggage.'

McLean intercepted the porter and asked him if Mr Severac was in his bedroom.

'Yes, sir. He will be down in a few moments. The taxi is to take him to London Airport.'

'Please take the baggage back,' said McLean. 'I will see Mr Severac in his room.'

Severac was just leaving his room when he saw McLean and Brook following his returned baggage. The porter dumped the two suitcases in the room, and McLean closed the door on him.

'I have to ask you some questions, Mr

281

Severac,' said McLean. 'You told me you would be here for two more days.'

'Yes, but I found there was a cancelled seat on the Paris plane, and I decided to take it.'

'You have told me where you were at eight-thirty on the night when Lescaut was killed, but will you tell me where you were from seven-thirty onwards?'

'I – I was walking the streets. I met nobody I know.'

'I suggest you saw Lescaut that evening.'

'No. Zat is not true,' protested Severac.

McLean then had the suitcases opened. Among the contents were several used shirts, and a spare suit. On the cuff of one of the shirts was a slight pinkish stain which McLean believed to be blood incompletely removed. The corresponding cuff of the suit showed similar imperfect treatment.

'What was it you tried to wash out from these two garments?' McLean asked.

'Nothing. I do not understand.'

'I think you do, Mr Severac. I am going to take you to police headquarters.'

Here Severac became violent, revealing himself as a man of uncontrollable passion, but his resistance was speedily overcome. In the car he dissolved into tears.

'You think I killed Lescaut,' he sobbed.

'Why should I – why?'

It was on the following day that McLean found a very good reason. He had been on the Paris telephone for hours at intervals and finally he breathed a sigh of relief.

'We have a good witness in Paris,' he said to Brook. 'He also is a musician. He swears that he was with Severac when he bought that copy of Lescaut's Sonata, and that Severac went almost mad with rage when he saw it. He swore that it was mainly his own work and that Lescaut must have stolen the unfinished manuscript from his studio shortly before he left France. The new witness also swears that Severac possessed an old Italian stiletto. I think our case now looks pretty convincing.'

16

The Two Pictures

I

The young woman with the large brown-paper parcel looked round a little awed as she entered the large reception hall at the Cavendish Museum, a few miles down the river at London, and the young man in attendance came to her aid with a smile.

'Can I help you, Madam?' he asked.

'Oh, thank you,' she said, blushingly. 'I have an appointment with the Curator.'

She put the parcel down for a moment and produced a letter which she handed to the young man.

'That's quite all right,' he said. 'I had better take you to his office. It is a little difficult to find.'

He led her through several long galleries, filled with pictures chiefly of maritime subjects, and models of ships in glass cases, finally to arrive at a door marked 'Curator'.

He rapped on the door, then entered and announced, 'Mrs Curtis, sir'. Then stood aside and closed the door after the visitor. The Curator, sitting at a desk, rose as the woman approached.

'Good morning!' he said. 'Do take a seat. Ah, those are the pictures you wrote about. Allow me.'

He laid the parcel on his desk, untied the string and exposed two very old oil paintings which he scanned one by one with considerable interest.

'Very nice,' he said finally. 'But I'm afraid they are not what you thought them to be. They are good work, and undoubtedly Dutch, but decidedly not Van der Velde.'

'Oh,' said Mrs Curtis. 'That's a little disappointing. I was told by a man who considers himself an expert that they might well be. But do you think they are of any considerable value?'

'We never attempt to value any picture submitted, but they are very well painted, but being unsigned makes all the difference. They are what are termed speculative. I wish I could help you more.'

'Well, it was very good of you to offer to see them,' Mrs Curtis said. 'It looks as if I shall not make a fortune after all.'

The Curator smiled and then wrapped the pictures up again and handed the parcel over to Mrs Curtis.

'I shall have to give you a pass out for the parcel,' he said. 'It's purely routine.'

He wrote the pass, signed it, and then escorted her to the door and wished her 'good day'. A little later she showed the pass to the young and admiring receptionist and went on her way.

Two hours later the Curator left his office and walked through the galleries to get his lunch. Half-way down the second gallery he stopped dead and gasped, for hanging on the wall, side by side, were the two pictures which Mrs Curtis had brought to show him. They replaced two excellent and valuable Van der Velde sea pictures which had undoubtedly been there when he arrived that morning. He almost ran into the office of the Director of the Museum.

'We've been robbed, Sir Henry!' he said. 'The two most valuable Van der Veldes in the whole collection.'

The Director looked very grim as the Curator related what had happened, and at the end of the narration he picked up the telephone and got in touch with Scotland Yard. Within half an hour Inspector McLean, accompanied by Sergeant Brook, were in the Director's office. The unhappy Curator was also present, and it was he who told McLean the full story, after which he handed McLean the letter which he had received from Mrs Curtis. It was to the effect that she had been informed that the Curator was always willing to give what information he could on old paintings of maritime subjects, by appointment, and that she had two paintings bequeathed to her which she thought might be Van der Veldes. Would he be kind enough to give her an appointment, preferably early in the morning. The address at the top of the letter was Marlborough Guest House, Gt Russell St. W.C.1.

'At what time did the woman arrive?' McLean asked.

'Half past ten. The museum opens at ten o'clock.'

'What was she like?'

'Quite young – perhaps about twenty-five years of age. On the slim side, with fair hair and blue eyes. She wore a kind of grey suit, and a tiny hat made of grey feathers. Very well spoken indeed.'

'I presume that at that time there were very few people in the galleries?'

'Scarcely anyone.'

'Were the two pictures which she brought already equipped with cord for hanging?'

'Yes.'

'Have you been in touch with the guest house?'

'Yes,' the Director cut in. 'I was informed that the woman had stayed there for a week, but had left two days ago.'

'By that time, I suppose, she would have received the letter from you giving her the appointment?' McLean asked the Curator.

'Yes. She would have received it a day before that. I get your point, Inspector, she used that guest house to give us a false address, and having got the appointment she moved out.'

McLean nodded and then took from the Director two postcard reproductions of the stolen paintings.

'Very nice,' he said. 'I see you have pencilled in the over-all dimensions. Are they insured?'

'Yes. Normally we do not insure our exhibits, but these paintings were part of a bequest, and insurance was conditional. Each is insured for £7,000.'

McLean then asked to have the loan of the substitute pictures and these were brought into the office. He examined them and saw how inferior they were to the stolen ones. Before he left McLean saw the receptionist who corroborated the description given by the Curator.

'Neat bit of work,' Brook commented when they were back in their car. 'Can't help admiring Mrs Curtis. Cute of her to get an early appointment, but she took a risk in making the substitution.'

'Yes, it was well planned,' McLean agreed. 'Now we'll pay a visit to that guest house, to see if there is anything to be learnt there.'

II

The lady who ran the guest house – a Mrs Meadows – was surprised by the police enquiry, for the Director of the museum had given her no inkling of what was in the wind.

'A very charming girl,' she said. 'I gathered that she had lost her husband abroad, and was looking round for some place to live in.'

'Did she receive any visitors during her stay?'

'Not to my knowledge.'

'Did she have a car?'

'No. She arrived in a taxi with just a single suitcase.'

'Did she receive any telephone calls?'

'Yes. Three of our bedrooms have telephone extensions. I think she had about four calls in all. Each time it was a man speaking.'

'Did she write her last address in your reception book?'

'No. She explained that she had only just arrived in England from South Africa.'

'Did she call a taxi when she left?' McLean asked.

'No. She said it wasn't far from the tube station, and from there she would go straight to Waterloo station.'

'I presume she paid the bill in cash?'

'Yes.'

McLean did not tarry for he wanted to get back to Scotland Yard to set some machinery in motion there, to stop the paintings from leaving the country. This done he took another good look at the two substitute pictures.

'Almost exactly the same size as the stolen pictures,' he ruminated. 'No doubt the thief measured up the Van der Veldes first and then looked round for two pictures of similar size, hoping that the substitution would not be noticed at once. That gives me an idea which might be worth trying out.'

McLean's idea was carried out the next day when several national newspapers carried reproductions of the two substitute pictures, asking for readers who might have seen them before, to communicate with the police. This was immediately successful, for round about noon a telephone call came through from a man named Andrews who ran an antique shop in Chelsea. He said he believed he had sold the pictures two weeks previously, and McLean asked him if he would come and have a look at them to make sure. He said he would and half an hour later he was in McLean's office.

'Good of you to come, Mr Andrews,' McLean said. 'Here are the paintings.'

Andrews did not hesitate for a moment.

'Yes,' he said. 'I bought them at a sale in Salisbury two months ago. I cleaned them up a bit and then showed them in my window. A fortnight ago a man came into the shop and asked me the price. We closed the deal at £25 the pair, and he took them away with him.'

'Did he pay cash for them?' McLean asked.

'Yes. I remember he gave me five five-pound notes.'

'A pity,' McLean said. 'That leaves me in

the blue. What was the fellow like?'

'Quite young – fair complexion. About six feet tall, and well turned out – quite Savile Row.'

'How did he remove the pictures?'

'Just carried them. He told me he had a car up the street at a parking meter.'

'Both the woman and the man covered up their tracks pretty well,' Brook commented later. 'But what beats me is how they intend to dispose of the loot. Surely nobody would buy two well-known paintings without finding out how the sellers came by them?'

'I hope you're right, Brook,' McLean said. 'But I must inform you that there are many cases on record where art treasures have been stolen and never seen again. That may well happen to the two Van der Veldes unless we move swiftly.'

But just where to move was a problem and McLean was cogitating on the matter when the Curator from the museum called on him, and was shown into his office immediately.

'I'm worried stiff over this business, Inspector,' he said. 'Couldn't sleep a wink last night. But I remembered something which I omitted to mention when you questioned me. When the woman brought her two pictures for me to see they were wrapped in a very large sheet of brown paper. I untied the string and opened the wrapper myself. On the underside of it there had been a label, but most of it had been torn off. All that was left were the words "Calshott & Win–'. Lying awake last night I recalled that there is a firm of high class tailors somewhere up west named Calshott and Wingate, and I wondered if the wrapper had originally been used to wrap up a box containing a suit. It was just an idea.'

'And a very good idea too,' McLean said. 'I am much obliged to you for the information, and will look into it at once.'

McLean found the name and address of the firm in the telephone directory and shortly afterwards he and Brook were in the office behind the large shop in consultation with the manager.

'I'll do all I can to help,' the manager said. 'But it's difficult for we post at least half a dozen suits every day, all of them specially tailored of course.'

'Well, the man I am interested in is young, six feet tall, and has ginger hair. You can't have many customers like that.'

'No, indeed. I'll get my cutter. He knows all our customers much better than I do.'

He excused himself and left McLean and Brook for a short time after which he returned with a very immaculate, elderly man who had a tape measure draped round his neck.

'We have a young gentleman customer with reddish hair, and very tall, Inspector,' he said. 'We made him a lounge suit recently and it was posted to him in one of our usual trade boxes. His name is George Creighton, and I believe he is the son of Sir Malcolm Creighton, the eminent lawyer.'

This caused McLean to raise his eyebrows for he had met the lawyer on two occasions.

'Where was the suit sent?' he asked.

'Flat number three, Wentworth Mansions, Bayswater.'

'Is he a married man?' McLean asked.

'Not to my knowledge. Some time ago I read in a newspaper that he had inherited a fortune from his grandmother.'

This looked as if McLean was on the wrong track, but he thanked the two men, and left them in complete ignorance of the nature of his enquiry.

'Doesn't sound too good to me,' Brook complained.

'Nor to me at the moment, but we'll follow it up. Drive to Wentworth Mansions.'

McLean had to call twice before he found George Creighton at home. He was a handsome, magnificently built fellow, round about twenty-five years of age, with charming manners. He led the callers into a beautifully furnished sitting-room, offered them chairs which they politely declined, and then asked what he could do for them.

'Mr Creighton, did you receive a parcel containing a new suit recently?'

'Yes. This happens to be the very suit,' Creighton said, with a smile. 'It's a very good suit too.'

'Have you the box in which it was packed?'

'Yes. It's rather a useful box, and I shoved it in my junk cupboard. Do you want to see it?'

'No, thank you. I am more interested in the paper wrapping. Is that also available?'

'I'm afraid not,' Creighton said. 'All garbage of that sort is put out daily for the rubbish collection. But was there anything special about the wrapper?'

'Yes, but if you have disposed of it there is nothing to be done about it. Excuse me asking, but are you a bachelor?'

'Very much so, and likely to be for a long time. I enjoy living alone.'

'You are fortunate in having such a nice home,' McLean said. 'Oh, there's just one more question. Did you recently buy two oil paintings from a dealer named Andrews in Chelsea?'

'No,' replied Creighton, looking surprised. 'Whatever made you think that?'

'I just wondered,' McLean said. 'Well, I won't take up any more of your time, and I'm sorry to have bothered you.'

'Not at all. I'm not a very busy person.'

III

'Innocent?' Brook asked as they left the building.

'As innocent as Charles Peace,' McLean replied. 'No doubt Andrews would be able to identify him, but I prefer to give him a little rope, because he is not the actual thief. By some means I have to track down the woman in the case, and I fancy that now he knows he is suspect he will make contact with his accomplice. I want you to hang around here and watch his movements until I can put a man on his track whom he doesn't know. I'll drive back to the Yard and bring Monkhouse back with me to relieve

296

you. Watch for me outside the church yonder.'

Brook was dropped and McLean went to headquarters and was soon back with Monkhouse. Brook saw the car arrive and came from where he had been loitering.

'No sign of him, Inspector,' he said.

'Good! You can take over from here, Bob,' he said to Monkhouse. 'You should be able to identify him quite easily. Very tall and athletic, with red hair. I'll leave you the car in case he should use his own car or call a taxi.'

This cat-and-mouse game went on for days. McLean now had two men working in relays and they made reports at intervals, the result of which showed Creighton to be leading the life of an idle and prosperous man-about-town. Much of his leisure was spent in various men's clubs, but several times he was observed to have dinner with a young couple of his own set. Monkhouse learnt that this pair were a Mr and Mrs Atherton of an address in Regent's Park. McLean made underground enquiries about them and found they were persons of unquestionable integrity. Mrs Atherton was a swarthy beauty and could not be confused with the mysterious Mrs Curtis who had hoodwinked the Curator.

The insurance company, facing a claim for £14,000, was now getting very restive. A fussy official came to see McLean to ask if any progress had been made, and McLean could only tell him that he still had hopes of finding the stolen paintings.

'You mean you have a suspect?' the official asked eagerly.

'Confidentially – yes, but I can't say more than that at this moment.'

The official looked a little relieved to have this assurance, but when he had gone Brook looked at McLean slyly.

'That was a bit optimistic, Inspector, wasn't it?'

'Just a little perhaps, but you can't expect me to say that I have abandoned all hope. I really do believe that the pictures are not far away. I don't think they were stolen to be resold, for young Creighton is a man of considerable wealth. I have definite inform-ation on that point. Despite the fact that he quarrelled with his family some years ago, none of his associates knows anything to his discredit.'

'Yet he lied to us,' Brook said.

'Yes. He had to in the circumstances, short of admitting complicity.'

It was some days later when Monkhouse telephoned McLean from Victoria station. He said that Mr and Mrs Atherton had picked up Creighton in a taxi, and the party had gone to Victoria station where they had been joined by another young woman, with fair hair and blue eyes. Monkhouse had stood behind Creighton at the booking-office and had heard him buy four tickets for Aldney, a small station at the back of Eastbourne. The train was due to leave in a quarter of an hour. What should he do.

'Hang on a minute or two,' McLean said, and then swiftly consulted a railway timetable.

He found that the train was a slow one, for the fast trains did not stop at the small station.

'You can come back to headquarters, Monkhouse,' he said. 'I'll take over now. I think I can beat that train to Aldney.'

A few minutes later he and Brook were on the road in a hundred-miles-an-hour car, and Brook enjoyed himself very much as they travelled eastward at tremendous speed. They reached Aldney five minutes before the train arrived, and from the station yard watched the quartet enter a waiting taxi. Ten minutes later the taxi entered a drive, and from the entrance McLean saw the party and their baggage enter the house. He got back into the car as the taxi emerged and passed them.

'Could be a wild-goose chase,' McLean said to Brook. 'But this appears to be Creighton's property, since he had a key to the front door.'

'Do we go in?' Brook asked.

'Give them a little time. I want to think out my next move. Have a cigarette.'

They sat and smoked for a few minutes, and then McLean got out of the car and peered up the drive towards the house. As he did so he saw Creighton go to a garage on the right of the house and emerge a little later in a small car which he drove to the front door. He then got out of it and entered the house, leaving the front door open. Soon he reappeared carrying a large square parcel which he put inside the car. McLean motioned to Brook to come forward, and as the police car reached the entrance gate McLean climbed inside.

'Drive right up,' he said. 'Creighton has just gone back into the house. I think he's about to make a journey.'

The police car pulled alongside the smaller vehicle, and McLean nipped out and took a look at the parcel. It was firmly packed and sealed and the label was addressed to the Curator, Cavendish Museum, London. Then Creighton appeared and stopped dead in his tracks as he saw McLean.

'I want to talk to you, Mr Creighton, and your guests,' McLean said. 'Take this parcel back with you, please.'

Creighton, now looking very pale and embarrassed took the parcel and McLean and Brook followed him into a large room where the Athertons and the other woman were helping themselves to drinks. McLean turned to the unknown woman.

'I believe you to be Mrs Curtis,' he said.

She looked appealingly at Creighton.

'She is an old friend of mine,' Creighton said, 'and her name is Olive Benson. At my instigation she did use the name Curtis on one occasion.'

'I must ask you to open this parcel,' McLean said.

Creighton produced a pocket-knife and cut the string. Inside were the two Van der Velde paintings, protected by layers of strawboard.

'So you were going to return them to the museum?' McLean said.

'Yes. They have been here all the time. We

had no intention of keeping them. It was a wager. We were all discussing the theft of another famous picture some weeks ago. I contended that it was easy to steal a picture from a picture gallery, because not enough precautions were taken. Atherton disagreed and dared me to have a shot at it. Finally I wagered him a hundred pounds that I and Olive would take those two pictures and hold them for fourteen days without being discovered. The time was up at noon today, and I have won my bet by a clear hour.'

'You may have won your bet, but you've won yourself something else at the same time, Mr Creighton. You'll learn exactly what that is when you are taken to court. Now I'll take the paintings with me and leave you to your somewhat untimely celebrations. Good day!'

The publishers hope that this book has given you enjoyable reading. Large Print Books are especially designed to be as easy to see and hold as possible. If you wish a complete list of our books please ask at your local library or write directly to:

Dales Large Print Books
Magna House, Long Preston,
Skipton, North Yorkshire.
BD23 4ND

Thi... ...or people
w... ...al print,
is p... ...uspices of

THE ... ...UNDATION

... w... ...yed this book.
Pleas... ...t about those
who... ...than you ...
an... ...read or enjoy
La... ...at difficulty.

... sending a
...mall, to:

...dation,
... Road,
A... ...E7 7FU,

or ... ...ure for

Th... ...onations
to ... ...visually
imp... ...ention
... ...gnosis

Than... you very much for your help.

DATE DUE